CW00433168

BRAMWELL

This is a Carlton Book

First published in Great Britain 1996
by Carlton Books,
20 St Anne's Court,
London W1V 3AW

10 9 8 7 6 5 4 3 2 1

Copyright © Carlton Books 1996

Cover photographs © Carlton UK Television Ltd

Bramwell is a Whitby Davison Production for Carlton © Carlton UK
Television Limited MCMXCVI

ISBN 0 7457 2681 8

All rights reserved.

This book is sold subject to the condition that it shall not, by way of
trade or otherwise, be lent, resold, hired out or otherwise circulated
without the publisher's prior written consent in any form of cover or
binding other than that in which it is published and without a similar
condition including this condition being imposed upon the
subsequent purchaser.

BRAMWELL

Sarah Jackson

Based on scripts by Lucy Gannon

CARLTON

Acknowledgements

Heartfelt thanks as always to Lorraine Dickey, my editor
at Carlton Books; and of course to my agent Robert Kirby
of Sheil Land Associates. Thanks also to Tim Whitby
and to all at Whitby Davison and the staff of Sheperton Studios for
their invaluable help. As for everyone else who ought to get a thank
you - if you don't know by now who
you are, I guess you never will.

Sarah Jackson is a pseudonym of Liz Holliday. Under her own name she has written novels of *Cracker* and *Bugs*; under the name of Lee O'Keefe she has written the novel of *Thief Takers*.

Her first love is science fiction, but she also writes crime. In 1989 she attended the Clarion Science Fiction Writers Workshop and hasn't looked back since. She has published SF, Fantasy and Crime stories, a stack of journalism and the storyboards and dialogue for several computer games. In 1994 her story 'And She Laughed' (London Noir, Serpents Tail) was nominated for the Crime Writers' Association Gold Dagger Award. She is an ex-youth worker, ex-theatre director and ex-teacher (among a whole lot of other things). She has no intention of becoming an ex-writer.

Chapter 1

Eleanor Bramwell's boots rang on the cobblestones in the square outside the East London Hospital. She looked to neither right nor left as she walked, and if she enjoyed the warmth of the summer sun on her neck, she showed no sign of it. She was about to watch an operation performed by Sir Herbert Hamilton, Chief Surgeon of the hospital. Medicine was the great love of Eleanor's life, but she loved it far too much ever to smile about it.

***

She marched through the receiving room, where the sick and injured sat huddled on long, wooden benches waiting to be seen. They brought their own smells to mingle with the carbolic and ether of the hospital: unwashed bodies and hair, rotgut beer and occasionally the sweet stink of mortifying flesh. Eleanor had long since learned to ignore the smell, but she had never quite become accustomed to it.

In the corner sat Roly, the deaf and blind son of the hospital cleaner. All day long he sat there in his place, locked in his dark and silent world, knowing nothing but the feeling of his body as he rocked back and forth, back and forth.

Eleanor walked past him, wishing for a moment that his sightless eyes would somehow see her; but it was useless. He

1

stared blindly at the wall and rocked, and all she could do was ignore him and go into the cloakroom. There, she took off her cloak and tied her apron over her street dress. Then she hurried out, down the corridor – past a man clutching a tiny baby and a boy leaning heavily on a makeshift crutch – and into the operating theatre.

Ten minutes later, she came out again and hurried into the courtyard. She stood with her back against the wall in the hot sun, sick to her stomach.

Sir Herbert came out. He was a tall man, red faced and with grey just beginning to salt his gingery hair. He had a temper to match his colouring. Not a man to cross. Eleanor's father had told her that repeatedly. He turned and glared at her for a moment, then went off patting his lips with his handkerchief as if he had just come from a fine meal.

She had witnessed a woman die under his scalpel – a woman who, in her opinion, should never have been operated on. Crimson arterial blood had spurted out from Sir Herbert Hamilton's botched incision, streamed over his hands, soaked into yards of wadding material, spattered the floor, and all the while the woman moaned quietly as the chloroform was too weak to hold her unconscious.

Not that Eleanor had really been able to hear her, for the cheers of the observing medical students had been too loud. They had taken bets on whether the woman would live or die. Some of them had won.

The woman, though – she had lost. She had lost because Sir Herbert had chosen to remove her ovaries, an operation he said would cure her of persistent melancholia.

I should have held my tongue, thought Eleanor. I should

have kept silent, knowing nothing I could say would change his mind. That, however, was not in her nature; and so she had told him what she thought. He had glared at her, as he had so many times before, and done exactly what he had intended to – as he had so many times before.

'Had enough for one day?' The voice, with its pronounced Scottish accent, came from behind Eleanor.

She turned. Doctor Joe Marsham, Sir Herbert's anaesthetist, was staring at her with a concerned expression. He was dark-haired and, Eleanor supposed, quite handsome if one were interested in that kind of thing, which she emphatically was not.

Doctor Marsham had always tolerated her presence far more easily than the other doctors had, perhaps because, unlike them, his origins were working class; therefore, he, like Eleanor, was something of an outsider. It would be sheer foolishness for Eleanor to snub one of her few allies.

'A perfectly healthy young woman lies dead,' she said. Her voice shook with rage, and she could only hope he would not notice.

'Melancholic,' Doctor Marsham said. 'Not perfectly healthy.'

'So if you're less than perfectly happy and fulfilled, we should chop off your testicles, Mr Marsham?'

It was a shocking thing to say, and Doctor Marsham was properly shocked. 'Doctor Bramwell!' She stared at him levelly. Then, suddenly, he smiled. 'And me a married man!'

'Do you think he'll do a ward round?' Eleanor asked, glancing in the direction Sir Herbert had taken.

'You're a glutton for punishment,' Doctor Marsham said, as he walked over to a bicycle that leaned against the wall nearby.

3

He wheeled it over to Eleanor. 'They'll never appoint a woman physician, much less a surgeon.'

'Oh but they will, one day.' Eleanor was certain of it. Sometimes, it was all that got her through the days. Mr Marsham just laughed. 'I didn't know it was yours,' Eleanor said, staring at the machine.

'My beautiful Bessie,' he answered. He pushed away from Eleanor and swung his leg over the saddle.

Eleanor watched as he bowled away across the square, marvelling at the freedom such a machine would give one.

***

Eleanor was sitting in the front parlour enjoying the late afternoon sun that shafted in through the tall windows as she read *The Lancet* when her father came in.

She glanced at her pocket watch. 'It's nearly six o'clock. I hope that's your last patient of the day.' There were guests coming to stay: the Chancellor of the Exchequer, no less, and his new young wife, who happened to be Eleanor's childhood friend Victoria. It really wouldn't do to be ill-prepared for them.

Father went over to the piano. He stood for a moment silhouetted against the window. Eleanor stared at him fondly. She supposed he was growing older, but to her he had always been the same: a tall, silver-haired gentleman with a short-clipped beard and moustache and amused blue eyes; although, as she had been told by her aunt often enough, there had been a time when those eyes had been filled with sorrow, for Eleanor's mother had died giving birth to her.

'It is,' Father said. 'That man was in a shocking state when he first came to me. Heart in a shocking state.' He bent and

4

picked out the first few notes of 'Abide With Me' with one finger. 'Lips blue. Hands shaking.' He glanced sharply at Eleanor. 'Private practice can be very satisfying...' Eleanor went back to her journal; this was an old debate and they had rehearsed the arguments many times, 'as you'd know if you left that hospital to work at home,' Father said, as if she were giving him all her attention.

Still, Eleanor never could resist rising to the bait. 'I'm not interested in spoilt ladies with imaginary ailments,' she said, though to be fair to Father, many of his patients had genuine illnesses.

Father laughed, sat down at the piano and played a trill. 'I saw my first spoilt lady at ten, my last poor gentleman at five,' he sang. 'In between I earned a small fortune,' he finished.

'Shameless!' Eleanor said, laughing.

Father brought his hands down hard, and a melodramatic chord or two thundered out. 'Certainly!'

'Not even a trace of guilt?'

'Not a jot,' Father declared, accompanied by another crashing chord. 'Wheel 'em in and rob 'em blind,' he said, scowling like a villain in a music hall play.

'You don't convince me, Father,' Eleanor said, putting down her journal. And indeed he didn't, for in Eleanor's opinion there was no finer physician in all England than Doctor Robert Bramwell – though she might, if pressed, admit to just a little bias.

Father played a tragic melody, one he'd no doubt heard on one of his many visits to the music hall. 'Go to your room, Miss, and turn yourself from a foul and common doctor into a lady.' He turned, as if to an imaginary audience. 'If she knows how…'

Eleanor stood up. 'An eighteen-inch waist and a fainting fit over the dessert?' she asked as she crossed the room. She stood behind Father. 'I think I can manage that,' she said and bent to kiss him on the cheek before she left the room to dress for dinner.

Behind her, her father continued to sing rather manically, 'I wheel them in and sit them down, I smile at them and say, "And how are you today, you're looking pale today"…'

Eleanor found herself smiling once again. Never had the tune to 'The Man Who Broke the Bank at Monte Carlo' been butchered to so little purpose.

A little later she stood before her mirror, brushing out her long chestnut hair, when she felt an ominous itching in her scalp. She rootled around in the mass of her hair. She found what she was looking for soon enough. She scowled at it. There were women, she supposed, who never scowled for fear of wrinkling their porcelain skin. Then again, they weren't the kind of women who got nits from working with paupers. She flicked the little beast across the room.

'Kate,' she shouted. 'Katie?'

Her ladies-maid scurried in, a little magpie of a girl in her black dress and white lace apron and mobcap. 'Yes, Miss Eleanor?'

'I've got them again, Kate,' she said without turning round.

In the mirror she saw the look of consternation on the maid's face. 'Oh,' Katie gasped. 'You haven't!' she said loudly, and with her usual candour.

'Shhh!' Eleanor urged. 'If Father knows he'll go mad.'

'He'll know soon enough – you'll have given them to all of us again,' Katie said. She hurried over to the washstand and began to prepare water to wash Eleanor's hair.

Botheration, thought Eleanor, pulling a face at her reflection in the mirror. Now she would be the one who was late for dinner.

***

'Oh, where is she?' Victoria's girlish voice rang out from the drawing room.

Eleanor hurried down the stairs, still fussing with the pins in her hair. 'Here I am,' she called and walked rather faster than was seemly into the room.

Victoria whirled round and grasped her hands. 'We're having a child – isn't that wonderful?' she said without preamble. She turned to her husband. 'Oh, tell them, Edward!'

Edward Carstairs smiled at Victoria, as a father might at an indulged child. He was much older than his wife, Eleanor noted, not quite able to approve, with hair that was just beginning to retreat and turn grey at the temples.

'You already have,' he said to Victoria. He turned to Eleanor's father. 'But we are.'

'Congratulations, my dear fellow.' Father pumped his hand warmly. 'I believe a small celebration might be in order. Eleanor, why don't you show Victoria upstairs and we'll see you at dinner?'

Eleanor smiled at the men. Usually, she would have joined her father in a pre-prandial drink, but she could see that on this particular occasion that would hardly be appropriate.

Chapter 2

Eleanor dabbed gently at Daniel Bentley's foot with a swab of lint dipped in lysol. His toes had been crushed by a Hansom cab and the little bones were broken and suppurating yellow pus.

Daniel gasped as she touched him. He could barely keep his foot still. She was trying to be gentle, but how could she possibly be gentle enough? Her task was not made easier by the way her mind kept straying to the conversation she had had with Victoria the night before. Victoria had spoken of an irritation that plagued her at night and begged Eleanor to examine her so that she might avoid, or at least prepare for, seeing Edward's own physician. It was probably unethical, or at least ill-advised, and Father was sure to be furious if he found out. Yet seeing Victoria's scared expression and noticing how pale she was, Eleanor had not been able to refuse.

She dabbed at an area of hardened yellow slough on Daniel's foot. It refused to move. An irritation, Victoria had said, that came to her in the night. Absently, Eleanor rubbed at Daniel's toe. He yelped. She glanced up at him where he lay in his hospital bed, one of several patients in the airy pavilion ward with its wide windows and swept wooden floor.

'If we could have some forceps, please Nurse,' she said. Next to her, Nurse Carr held a kidney bowl and guarded the instrument trolley as carefully as if it contained jewels.

'Doctor Bramwell,' Nurse Carr said, but she didn't hand over the forceps. She was a tall woman, big boned and hatchet faced, very sure of her authority here on the ward. Eleanor sometimes felt her disapproval as a tangible thing.

'Something to clean this slough away,' she insisted. She was used to the disapproval of the staff, and used to fighting her way through it.

'You're supposed to follow in my wake, not forge ahead of me, Miss Bramwell,' Sir Herbert's voice boomed out. Eleanor turned. Sir Herbert strode across the ward towards her, closely followed by Doctor Marsham. Nurse Carr moved back out of the way with a hastily repressed told-you-so expression on her face. It seemed Eleanor had misjudged her intent. Eleanor decided she would have to remember that in the future.

But now she must pacify Sir Herbert. She got up quickly and faced him. His gingery hair appeared copper in the early morning sun and contrasted starkly with his black frock coat. 'Sir Herbert,' she said, gesturing at Daniel's injured foot. 'I was just cleaning it.'

He bent over the bed to examine the foot, tutting to himself. Eleanor couldn't resist glancing over Sir Herbert's back to Doctor Marsham. He smiled at her, but she knew he must be thinking she deserved all she got.

Sir Herbert prodded carefully at the wound. Daniel's lips peeled back from his teeth in an agonized grimace, and he let out his breath in a sustained hiss. Sir Herbert didn't seem to notice. 'Well I dare say you women have a gentler touch than we men,' he said. 'And when I operate, I'll have clean flesh to work on.' Daniel shot Eleanor a terrified glance. Sir Herbert stood up. 'We'll have this foot off, shall we?' he asked Daniel, who looked in fear of his life.

It was exactly what Eleanor had feared Sir Herbert would suggest. She had been determined to keep silent, but seeing Daniel's frightened face it was more than she could do.

'Sir Herbert!' she said. Doctor Marsham pulled a face at her that very clearly told her she should, in his opinion, stifle her objections. Well, she never had been one for listening to the opinions of others. She plunged on, ignoring him. 'I've never had the opportunity to treat a crush injury,' she said. Sir Herbert glared at her from under his sandy eyebrows. 'I wondered...might I attempt the care of this patient?'

'You're not suggesting that you take over my theatre?' he demanded.

'If you would allow it...' Eleanor faltered in the face of his fixed stare. 'I would like to remove just the affected toes.' Sir Herbert didn't respond. Eleanor swallowed hard. 'Here,' she said, hoping to mollify him. 'Try to save the foot,' she added by way of explanation.

Sir Herbert looked at the floor. 'Flying in the face of scientific knowledge again, Miss Bramwell?'

'I know the risks,' Eleanor said, praying she didn't sound arrogant. 'But if you would trust me...'

Sir Herbert stared at her appraisingly for a moment or two. Then he glanced at Daniel's foot. 'Oh I dare say you'll do well enough.' It was as much of a compliment as she was ever likely to get from him, and more than she had ever expected. She stopped herself from smiling just in time. 'Nurse,' Sir Herbert continued, 'I hand Mr...' he walked round the bed so that he could see the card pinned on the wall above it, 'Bentley over to the ministrations of this young woman.' Nurse Carr, who had been standing silently all this time, smiled thinly. Daniel Bentley, meanwhile, looked quite as appalled at this idea as he had at the news of having his foot removed. Sir Herbert turned to him and winked. 'Don't worry, I'll keep an eye on you.' He laughed and swept out, without waiting for Doctor Marsham or Eleanor to follow him. 'Thank you, Sir,' Daniel said to his retreating back. He didn't seem much reassured.

Doctor Marsham turned to Eleanor. 'He's in a wonderful mood,' he said. That explains quite a lot, Eleanor thought. She should have known better than to ascribe her success to the quality of her work. 'Lady Cora Somebody-or-other is giving him a ward,' Doctor Marsham went on.

'Lady Cora Peters,' Eleanor said, remembering something her father had said a few days before. 'One of the Berkshire Peters. Her husband's left two hundred a year for the benefit of the poor.' She went over to the trolley, to continue cleaning Daniel's foot.

Doctor Marsham started to follow Sir Herbert. As he passed her he said drily, 'What elevated circles you move in.' Eleanor found she wasn't sure whether or not he was teasing her.

Before she could say anything, Daniel Bentley said, 'I don't mind him chopping off me foot, Miss, if it needs chopping.'

'I don't mind him chopping off your foot if it needs chopping,' she said, walking towards the bed. 'And I'm a doctor, not a miss.' She smiled at him slightly, to soften it. 'I'll see you tomorrow,' she said and walked off before he could protest.

If only, she thought as she walked through the ward, if only she could be as confident about the outcome of her examination of Victoria.

Chapter 3

Eleanor dried her hands on the towel by the washstand in the guest bedroom. She was not at all sure how to tell Vicky what she had discovered.

'Of course, Edward says he doesn't mind which it is, but a boy would be nice from the point of view of an heir,' Vicky said from behind her.

Eleanor turned slowly. Vicky was sitting on the edge of the bed, doing up the last few hooks of her corset. 'Victoria,' she said. She smoothed down the skirt of her coffee-and-cream street dress, wondering how to continue.

'Victoria?' Vicky said archly. 'I am impressed. You sound just like a doctor.' She giggled.

Eleanor put the towel aside. 'I'm sorry,' she said. 'I'm so sorry.' Vicky's smile faltered. It was obvious to Eleanor that she didn't understand. 'You aren't having a baby,' she said gently. Vicky's eyes widened in shock. If only that were the worst of it, Eleanor thought. She crossed the room to her friend. She had to be certain Vicky understood. 'You're not carrying a child.' Vicky's eyes filled with tears.

'You're sure?' she whispered.

'I'll get you a glass of water,' Eleanor said. It was inadequate, but it was all she could think of. She crossed to the bedside table and filled a glass from the carafe that stood by the gaslamp.

'I must be, I can feel it!' Vicky's voice was a wail of desperation.

'When you long for a child, you can convince yourself,' Eleanor said. It hardly answered Vicky's desperation, but it was the best she could do.

She put the glass down on the table, realizing that she had poured it more to give herself something to do than to help Vicky. Her hands were shaking.

'Edward will be so disappointed,' Vicky said. Her voice was thick with tears.

Eleanor went to sit next to her on the bed. 'He'll get over it,' she said, hating the forced optimism in her voice. 'He's besotted with you.' That, at least, was true.

'Now, yes,' Vicky said. 'But he can be so distant.' Her face was a mask of misery. One part of Eleanor was surprised that her friend had even that much insight; another wondered if she ought – if she dared – to tell her the other thing she had discovered, considering how badly she was taking this. 'Oh God,' Victoria said. Her face was a mask of despair. 'I've failed him.'

'You haven't,' Eleanor said impatiently. She caught herself and moderated her tone. 'Vicky, this isn't your fault.'

'We've been married six months!'

'Six months is nothing.' Eleanor took Vicky's hand in her own.

'Edward is forty-five,' Vicky said. 'I'm useless at everything I do…' Her voice trailed off and she looked away. The lamplight turned her fair skin almost translucent.

'Don't,' Eleanor commanded. 'Vicky, don't blame yourself like this.'

'I thought this was the one thing I could manage,' Vicky said. Her face crumpled and for a moment she sat and sobbed. 'It's no wonder he humours me as if I were a child.' Her voice rose, verging on hysteria. 'He's so good and clever and I'm so…'

Good! thought Eleanor. Listening to her friend almost deify a man who had treated her so shabbily was more than she could bear. 'Victoria, listen to me,' she cut in. 'This isn't your fault,' she repeated. She took a deep breath. Vicky stared at her out of dark, pain-filled eyes. 'He's given you an infection,' Eleanor said. There was no going back now, she realized, even though Vicky still didn't seem to understand. 'He's given you syphilis.' She searched her friend's face for some sign of understanding but found none. 'Do you understand what syphilis is?' she asked softly. Victoria shook her head dumbly.

Gently, Eleanor explained, and equally gently held Vicky until the storm of tears subsided and she lay exhausted on the bed. Some of her dark hair had come down from its pins, and it fanned out across the crisp whiteness of the pillow-case.

'Some people say the disease lies forever dormant,' she explained, more to be saying something than because she thought it would help. 'Others that…' Vicky turned her head away. Her face was coated with tears that glistened like crystal in the soft gaslight. 'Vicky,' Eleanor said urgently, 'new discoveries are being made about syphilis every day. Really.'

Vicky blinked slowly. 'So I caught it from Edward,' she said. 'And how did he get it?'

Eleanor stared at her helplessly. There was no easy

14

answer. 'That's difficult,' she said, striving to find a delicate way of putting it. 'The same way.'

A look of horror spread across Vicky's face as she finally came to understand what Eleanor had been trying to tell her all this time.

'I know,' Eleanor said. 'But a man of Edward's age isn't a virgin.' Vicky looked disgusted, and for a moment Eleanor was sure she would start to cry again. 'Forget how he got it, Vicky,' she urged. 'Think about the future.' To her horror, she heard the voice of Lady Cora Peters booming out downstairs. Eleanor wondered if she were the first of their guests or merely the loudest. 'There are treatments,' she said, horribly aware that soon she would have to go downstairs. She was, after all, her father's hostess. 'I'll find out everything I can about the latest thinking,' she said, wondering how Vicky would react when she realized that she, too, would have to go downstairs and face Edward.

As if on cue, the door handle turned. The door was locked, so it did not open, but a moment later there came a gentle knocking. 'Victoria?' It was Edward's voice. 'It's me.'

Victoria licked her lips. 'I can't,' she whispered. 'I can't.' Her hand clutched at the bedclothes beside her.

Eleanor got up and went to the door.

'Open the door, darling,' Edward said from the other side.

Eleanor scowled at him through the dark wood of the door. Then she opened it a crack.

Edward was wearing his dinner jacket, but his collar was undone. 'I can't do my tie,' Edward said, as she came out. He stopped when he realized he was not speaking to Vicky. Eleanor closed the door behind her so that Edward could not see in.

'I'm sorry, Edward,' Eleanor said quickly. 'Vicky's not well.'

'She's not well? What's the matter with her?' He started to go past Eleanor but she put her hand on the door knob to prevent him.

'She's very upset,' Eleanor said, wondering how much she would be forced to say. 'She won't be at dinner.'

Edward stared at her for a moment. 'Nonsense,' he said at last. 'She was fine this…' He caught himself, and a look of consternation passed across his fine-chiselled features. 'The child!' he exclaimed. 'She's not lost the child?'

To give him his due, he did seem upset; though Eleanor could not help wondering if it were more at the thought of the loss of a possible heir, despite Vicky's protestations that he did not care about the sex of the baby, than at the thought of harm coming to Vicky.

'There was no child,' she said, keeping her voice low so that Vicky would not hear her and become overwrought again.

'Oh God,' Edward said. The colour had drained from his cheeks. 'She's not miscarried, has she?' His voice wavered.

Eleanor took a deep breath, suddenly unable to control the wave of revulsion and anger which swept through her. 'No,' she said levelly. 'You didn't give her a child.'

She glared at Edward, challenging him to meet her gaze. A muscle jumped in his jaw.

'I see,' he said.

Again he started to go into the room, and again Eleanor barred his way. 'Victoria doesn't want to see you,' she said and then, seeing that his upset seemed genuine, added more gently, 'She's in tears, very distressed. Please tell

Father I'll be down directly.'

'You haven't told her?' Edward demanded, and Eleanor realized that what she had taken for upset was actually the ice-cold chill of his anger.

'Surely you realized you were putting her in danger?' she retorted, and immediately regretted it: not because she felt she should not have challenged him but because she sounded so defensive.

'What have you told my wife?' His voice was razor sharp.

'The guests are waiting.' To say more would have been to give in to her own white-hot fury. She slipped back into the bedroom without waiting to see if he went downstairs.

Vicky was staring listlessly at the wall. Eleanor sat down on the bed next to her again.

Vicky turned to look at her. 'Edward?' she asked.

'I've told him you're not feeling well,' Eleanor said. It wasn't quite a lie. 'I don't expect he'll bother you tonight.'

'Thank you,' Vicky said. She took Eleanor's hand. 'You're a good friend.' Tears started in her eyes. 'A good friend,' she repeated.

Eleanor smiled. 'So are you,' she said. She glanced at the pocket watch pinned to the bodice of her dress. It was well past seven. 'I'm afraid I have to go, now. I believe Lady Peters has already arrived.' Vicky's hand closed around hers. 'I'll come back, afterwards, I promise,' she said. 'You should try to sleep.'

'I can't,' Vicky said, and for a moment Eleanor thought she would cry again.

Eleanor stood up. 'Try,' she said. 'You'll feel better.'

Vicky nodded but she did not look convinced.

Eleanor left her then and went to change – with great haste –

for dinner. By the time she got downstairs, Edward, Lady Peters and Father were waiting for her, along with the rest of the guests.

Lady Peters was a handsome, apricot-haired woman in her late forties, just beginning to run to plumpness; her dress, though mourning-black, was the height of fashion and sparkled dully with thousands of tiny jet beads at the neckline and hem. They were overmatched, though, by the diamonds that glittered at Lady Peters' ears, wrists and throat. Eleanor, in her favourite moiré silk dress felt almost dowdy by comparison.

'How is my poor sister-in-law?' she asked, almost as soon as Eleanor walked into the room.

Edward shot her a fierce glance. 'She is…indisposed and needs to rest,' Eleanor said, guardedly. 'I'm sorry to have kept you all waiting,' she went on. 'We should eat, before the food spoils.'

'Yes, let's do,' Father said, coming to her rescue. 'I'm famished, and besides Kate will have my life if we take much longer.'

There was a scatter of laughter and the guests – five more besides Lady Peters and Edward – moved through into the formal dining room, where the table was covered in crisp white damask and laden with silver and crystal that picked up and multiplied the light from the candles. Eleanor's father sat at one end of the table, with Eleanor facing him, while the guests found their nameplates and seated themselves.

The food arrived, and the conversation wended its way from the politics of the day – on which subject Edward was voluble – to the inevitable gossip.

It was during the fish course that Lady Peters said, 'My

husband left a property in Thrift Street and a small trust fund to benefit the poor and sick, and suddenly every doctor I meet', she turned and nodded with an ironic smile to Eleanor's father, '– apart from you Robert – has a worthy cause to support.'

Father smiled mischievously. 'We're a rotten lot, we doctors.' His blue eyes sparkled in the candlelight. 'Apart, that is, from my daughter, who devotes herself entirely to the East London Hospital and never considers money,' he said, to the amusement of the guests and somewhat to Eleanor's embarrassment.

Lady Peters turned to her, making the gemstones in her pendant earrings bob and glitter. 'You remind me so much of your mother,' she said, and suddenly the frivolity of the conversation was lost, at least for Eleanor. 'She was a strong character, too.' She turned to Father to say, 'Wasn't she, Doctor Bramwell?' Before he could answer, she said to Eleanor, 'Such a pity you never knew her.'

'I have her portrait,' Eleanor said, wistfully. It was all she had, for she had no memory at all of her mother.

'She was so exquisite, so wonderful,' Lady Peters said.

'Yes, she was,' Father murmured as if lost in memory. Eleanor found herself unaccountably melancholy. Then he seemed to catch himself. 'And headstrong, and determined,' he said, and was his usual jovial self once more.

'She would be very proud of you, I'm sure,' Lady Peters said to Eleanor, as if she realized that she had dampened the mood. 'It must be very difficult work.'

'Not really,' Eleanor said, deciding that she could think about Mother later, if she still felt like it. 'They allow me to do so little. But I hope…' She faltered, as a movement at the top of the stairs caught her attention. Victoria, dressed in her

19

outdoor coat and carrying her valise, was making her way down. Edward must have seen the look of horror on her face for he followed the direction of her gaze. She stumbled to a conclusion, 'to get a job one day.' Even as she finished the sentence she was standing up.

So was Edward. 'If you'll excuse me,' he said dabbing his lips with his napkin.

He strode out. Eleanor followed him, pausing only to say, 'Do continue,' to the guests.

Edward's voice came from the hall. 'And where are you going?' he demanded.

Eleanor hurried out. She turned at the doors and said, 'Excuse me.' Then she backed out, closing the doors behind her.

'Let me go!' shouted Vicky.

Eleanor whirled round. Edward had grabbed Vicky. She jerked against his grip, trying to get free; but it was useless. Tears streamed down her face. Meanwhile, Kate watched it all impassively.

'I forbid you to leave this house,' Edward said. 'You're hysterical.' He shook Vicky as if she were a child. 'Go to your room.'

Eleanor picked up her skirts and ran over to them. 'It's late. Where will you go?' she said to Vicky, hoping her urgency would get through. 'You've no cab fare.'

Edward rounded on her. 'Keep out of it.' He shook Victoria by the hand again. 'We'll talk about this in the morning.'

'I won't stay,' Vicky protested. She tried to shake him off but he was far too strong. 'It keeps going round in my head,' she pleaded to Eleanor, her voice getting louder and more shrill with every word. 'How he must have caught this foul thing.'

'Shut up,' Edward hissed at her. He turned to Kate and shoved her hard. 'Get me her key.' She didn't move fast enough, so he pushed her again. 'Get me her key!'

Kate ran off and Edward began to drag Vicky to the stairs. She yanked at his arm but couldn't break free. 'How could you do this to me?' she implored, trying at least to stop him pulling her along.

'I've done nothing,' Edward said. Eleanor wondered if he believed it. 'You're making a fool of yourself,' he went on as they reached the stairs.

Eleanor looked up at them, appalled. 'You can't lock her in!' she exclaimed.

Edward did not stop. 'You'd have her roam the streets, would you?' Vicky stumbled up the stairs after him.

Eleanor followed them. 'Don't worry, Vicky, I'll sit with you,' she said, knowing it sounded pathetic. Edward stopped. He turned and glared down contemptuously at Eleanor. 'Edward,' she said, 'do return to the guests.' His face was impassive. 'Please. I promise you, she'll not go anywhere.'

Edward dropped Vicky's hand. 'Then mind what you say,' he said. He pushed past them. 'Keep your dangerous little knowledge to yourself.' He clattered down the stairs, back to the dining room. Eleanor put her arm round Vicky. 'Shh,' she said. 'Hush now, it's all right…' She only wished it were really so.

**

Later, after Vicky had finally fallen into an uneasy, tear-drenched sleep, Eleanor heard the chatter of voices and the clatter of carriages in the road as the guests started to leave. She went over to the bedroom window to watch them go. Well, they would have something to gossip about now, she supposed, as she twitched the Belgian lace curtains back into place.

And as for herself, now she would have to go down and face Edward again. And Father.

***

Eleanor clutched a glass of whisky as she faced them in the drawing room. 'I didn't intend to tell her,' she said, knowing she sounded defensive. Well, perhaps the best defence was to be on the offensive, and since they already felt she'd offended so gravely, she hardly had anything to lose by it. 'She was blaming herself when the blame lay with someone else.' She directed her words to Edward but it was Father who looked affronted. 'She didn't get it from the sheets, Father!' Before he could respond, she turned to Edward and ploughed on, 'You must have known you had syphilis.'

His hands clenched and unclenched. 'Had it and was cured of it,' he said stiffly.

'Whom did you consult?' Father asked, in his best professional manner.

Edward's jaw worked. 'Several good men,' he said at last, directly to Eleanor's father. 'I was advised to wait two years until the symptoms had subsided. I did.' He paused, then, still not looking at Eleanor, went on, 'Contrary to your obvious opinion, I care about her deeply.'

Father put his hand on Edward's shoulder. 'Edward, I'm sorry,' he said.

Eleanor pursed her lips in a burst of irritation that took her quite by surprise. It was not often that she disagreed with Father's assessment of a situation. Well, perhaps it wasn't that rare, she thought honestly; but it wasn't often she found herself minding that she disagreed quite so much.

'Well, it's not the end of the world,' Edward said, suddenly loud, as if he'd decided to brazen it out. 'It will not last for ever!' He spun round, including Eleanor in the conversation again. 'For God's sake, you're making a great issue out of this.'

It was more than Eleanor was prepared to listen to. 'And what if she had been pregnant?' she demanded. 'Have you any idea what her syphilis could have done to the baby?' She glared at him, but he didn't answer. 'Tell him!' she commanded Father; but he, too, was silent. 'We have a boy who comes to the hospital every day. His mother sits him in the reception hall while she washes the floor. He's deaf. He's blind. He's unable to understand anything but the food in his mouth and a hand leading him. His mother had syphilis when she conceived him.' She stopped, quite breathless with anger.

Edward looked away from her. As well he might, she thought. He crossed to the side table to pour himself another drink.

Eleanor went on, 'But even if Victoria avoids childbirth, there can be terrible consequences.'

'That's enough,' Edward snapped. 'I shall do whatever I can for my wife, and I shall do it without your interference.' He didn't give Eleanor a chance to interrupt. 'I shall get her the best medical care available – without the terrible distress you've caused her.' He turned to Father. 'I trust you'll ensure this matter goes no further?'

'Yes, of course.' Father scowled at Eleanor, who found herself wilting under his gaze like a naughty schoolgirl. 'You have our word.'

'Thank you,' Edward said. 'I'll take yours.' He slammed his

glass down on the table and strode across the room.

Father bade him goodnight from the doorway. 'Goodnight, Edward. I'm so very sorry.' He stood there for a moment but he did not get an answer. When he came back into the room, he shut the door with such great care that Eleanor knew he was furious.

She sat down on the sofa. 'I had no choice, Father,' she said. 'I did it for the best.'

'Had you no thought for her emotional vulnerability?' There was ice in Father's gaze.

'Rather more than her new husband has, obviously,' Eleanor snapped back.

'You had no business examining her in the first place and, having done so, you had no right to tell her what you did,' Father shouted.

Eleanor felt the colour drain from her face. Her grip tightened on the cut crystal of her whisky glass. She was not used to him raising his voice. 'Someone had to tell her,' she shouted back.

'Yes, but not you.' Father glared at her for a moment then lowered his voice, seemingly by an effort of will. 'You should have spoken to me, managed the whole thing so much better.' For a moment Eleanor thought his anger had dissipated. Then suddenly he was furious again. 'Good God, Eleanor,' he said, 'he could have you struck off for this.'

He was right. It wasn't something she had even considered. 'And risk his reputation?' she said, but she could hear the desperation in her own voice.

'And Victoria's! That is what you're playing with here, Miss!' Two red spots appeared high on his cheeks. 'One

24

word of this and her life will be changed forever. His life, his career too.'

Oh yes, Eleanor thought, of course the damage to Edward would be more important than anything that might happen to Vicky. 'Her life is changed!' she said fiercely. 'Vicky may never be cured.'

She was right. She could see it in his eyes and in the fact that he did not even try to answer. Say something, she thought at him, make it right between us. She would have said something herself but everything she thought of would only have made it worse.

After a moment he strode to the door; but before he got there, he turned to her. 'Don't always assume you are the only one who cares,' he said. She stared at her whisky, schooling herself to silence. 'Edward will do everything he can for her, as will her physician. Let's just hope they do it with a little more understanding than you've just shown.' Then he went, leaving Eleanor alone.

How will they show more understanding? she wondered. By lying to her, perhaps? By telling her that in a year or two the symptoms would subside, when the truth was that no-one knew if the disease ever truly left the body.

Father had said she shouldn't assume she was the only one who cared. Well, she thought, when others act as if they do, perhaps I'll change my mind. But not until then.

Chapter 4

Eleanor tried not to look at Roly next morning. She did not succeed. His blind eyes seemed to stare at her as she walked past him in the receiving room. His skin was pasty and livid with scratches, where, she supposed, he had clawed at himself.

That Vicky could have such a child was unthinkable – and that, of course, was the problem. They would far rather not think about it, and not let her think about it either. She put it out of her mind. Today, she was a doctor. A surgeon, no less, and Daniel Bentley was her only concern.

She put on a heavy calico apron over her street dress and went to the ward. Nurse Carr had already prepared Daniel and brought in a trolley of instruments. Doctor Marsham arrived a moment after Eleanor. He prepared quickly, and then there was nothing for it but to do the operation.

She glanced over at the bed. Daniel lay quietly, with his leg strapped to the bed under a wire hoop covered with a blanket, but he looked terrified and his breath came in short, hard gasps.

'I'll give him the cocaine now,' Doctor Marsham said, 'but you must be ready to cut in two minutes. No later,' he added warningly. Eleanor nodded. Her mouth was dry with fear. I wanted this, she thought. I've always wanted this. 'It'll numb the pain, but not for long, so be quick,' Doctor Marsham said.

Eleanor nodded again. Perhaps her nervousness showed more than she hoped it did, for he laid a gentle hand on her shoulder. Eleanor felt her eyes go wide with surprise. Doctor Marsham added, 'You'll be fine.'

Eleanor broke away and turned to the bed. 'Right, Nurse,' she said. Her voice sounded appallingly loud and far too cheerful. 'Please remove the dressing.'

'I've done it, Miss Bramwell,' Nurse Carr said, as if she expected praise. She pulled the blanket off the hoop frame, revealing Daniel's naked foot, which was covered with newly formed scabs despite the cleaning Eleanor had done the day before.

Daniel Bentley sat up and stared at them in terror, like a man brought face to face with his executioners.

'I spent an hour cleaning it yesterday, and today you cover it with a dirty blanket,' said Eleanor, exasperated.

'The blankets are washed every month, Miss,' Nurse Carr said stiffly. Her face showed what she thought of being reprimanded by another woman.

'Doctor,' Eleanor snapped. She glared at Nurse Carr for a moment. 'Right,' she said. 'We'll just have to wash it again.'

Nurse Carr snatched the hoop away with a sulky tip of her chin.

Doctor Marsham went over to Daniel. 'Mr Bentley,' he said, handing him a small brown bottle of gin. 'Another drink, please.'

Daniel swigged from the bottle, then wiped his mouth with the back of his hand. Colour rose in his cheeks.

'Lysol and lint, please,' Eleanor said. Nurse Carr brought them over in an enamel dish, and Eleanor swabbed Daniel's foot, ignoring his grunts of pain. 'Please, Doctor Marsham?' she said when she had finished.

Doctor Marsham came over, carrying a syringe full of cocaine. He held it up to the light and pushed the plunger so that a droplet or two seethed out from the needle.

'Is the knife ready, Nurse?' Eleanor asked.

'Is that knife sharp, Miss?' Daniel asked. 'Only it wants to be sharp.' His eyes were very large. Doctor Marsham slammed the needle into the crushed part of his foot. He howled in pain and his body snapped back against the bed. 'Bleedin' needle ain't,' he gasped. His lips skinned back from his teeth.

Eleanor looked at him. Somehow it was easier that he didn't quite trust her. If it went wrong…but she would not think like that. This was it, the moment she had worked so hard for, and no matter that it wasn't in a proper operating theatre.

Eleanor picked up the scalpel. Daniel pushed himself up, and when he saw the knife, took another drink of gin. Doctor Marsham hurried to the head of the bed and pushed Daniel's shoulders down. He looked round and nodded for Eleanor to proceed. Eleanor traced out the line of the amputation. A crimson line marked the scalpel's trail.

'Poor little piggies,' Daniel said, slurring his words. 'Plates of meat. This little piggy went to market.'

'The black knife, Nurse,' Eleanor said, trying to ignore him. She took a good deep breath and prayed she'd be able to keep a steady hand.

'Only one plate of meat from now then, eh? Or one and a half. Enough for a working man.'

Eleanor cut down hard, knowing that gentleness now would be a false kindness. Blood spurted out round the scalpel.

Daniel gasped. 'This little piggy…' he was breathing hard now, 'stayed home.'

The scalpel crunched on bone. Eleanor leaned into the cut with all her weight. Daniel screamed and bucked as the pain hit him even through his cocaine-fogged senses.

'You cow!' Daniel gasped.

'Now now, nearly done,' Doctor Marsham said.

'This little piggy had…' gasped Daniel as Eleanor cut the last thread of flesh and skin, 'none.'

Eleanor threw the gobbets of ragged flesh into a bucket, where they sat like so many pieces of ox-tail on a butcher's slab.

Daniel, released by Doctor Marsham, sat up. He looked at the bloody stub of his truncated foot and started cheering. ''Kin 'ell,' he said. Eleanor pretended not to have heard him. 'This little piggy was gone.' He spread his arms wide and started to sing some tuneless nonsense.

Eleanor stared down at her handiwork. Nurse Carr, having recovered from her snit, handed her a needle and catgut.

'Lovely job,' Doctor Marsham said. He shot an amused glance at Daniel. 'Gin and laudanum,' he said, smiling, 'as used by the best poets and men of letters.'

'You can start now, Milady,' Daniel interrupted. 'I'm ready.'

Eleanor held up the needle. It glinted wickedly in the morning light. 'All done, Mr Bentley,' she said. 'Just the embroidery.'

Doctor Marsham went to hold him down again. 'Nice bit of bodery,' Daniel said, stumbling over the word. Eleanor thrust the needle into his skin. He screamed and clutched at Doctor Marsham, making the catgut jerk and hurt him further. Eleanor tugged on the thread to free it.

'How are you getting on, Doctor Bramwell,' came Sir Herbert's voice from beside her shoulder.

Eleanor had been too engrossed in her work to hear him approach. 'I've nearly finished, Sir,' she said without looking round. 'I've removed three toes.' She glanced round and saw that Lady Peters was with him, her widow's black lightened today by a jaunty straw hat with a purple ribbon. Good. Perhaps he would be less rude than usual with her there. She tugged at the catgut again, trying to pull it tight so she could knot it off.

Daniel yelped. 'Tie a button on it, do,' he yelled. He waved the bottle around. It flew from his hand and smashed against the floor so that the sweet smell of gin mingled with that of lysol and carbolic. Lady Peters looked at him in dismay. He called, 'Buggering about all sodding day.' Eleanor finally managed to knot the thread off. Daniel's back arched. 'Shit!' he screamed.

Lady Peters gasped. Out of the corner of her eye, Eleanor saw the older woman's hand go to her mouth.

'Fresh air, Lady Peters,' Sir Herbert said and, to Eleanor's great relief, helped her away.

It took Eleanor only a few more moments to finish what she was doing and instruct Nurse Carr how to tend Daniel. Then she and Doctor Marsham left the ward together.

Sir Herbert was sitting outside, paying close attention to Lady Peters. As Eleanor started to go past, she heard the older woman say, '...to become involved, to do some good.' Sir Herbert nodded his head and seemed about to say something when Lady Peters looked away from him. 'Miss Bramwell!' she called out. 'That poor man.'

'He's a very lucky man.' Doctor Marsham contradicted her

before Eleanor could say anything. 'Doctor Bramwell's saved his foot.' It was much more than Eleanor would have dared in front of Sir Herbert.

'We hope,' he said, smiling tightly. 'This young lady has novel ideas about medicine and surgery.'

'I just try to preserve whatever's healthy,' Eleanor said, hoping she did not sound too provocative. She knew Sir Herbert would never forgive her if she made him look foolish or mean-spirited in front of Lady Peters.

Sir Herbert stood up between Eleanor and Lady Peters. 'The important thing is you were given the opportunity to try,' he said, and Eleanor took it for a warning. 'To learn.' His expression made very clear what lesson he hoped she would take from the morning's activities. He turned back to Lady Peters, evidently considering the matter closed.

'And that Mr Bentley will return to work,' Eleanor said. There was the slightest, the very slightest, tremor in her voice. 'He has a large family.'

Sir Herbert dismissed that. 'They all have large families.' He put out a hand to Lady Peters. 'My dear lady, let me help you.'

He, in turn, was dismissed with a wave of Lady Peters' hand. 'Herbert, I felt queasy. I'm not an invalid.' She went over to Eleanor. 'I do hope you find a position in this hospital, Eleanor,' she said and turned to Sir Herbert. 'Perhaps in my new ward?'

Sir Herbert managed to look only slightly nonplussed. 'Perhaps, perhaps,' he said. 'Who knows?' He took Lady Peters' elbow and steered her down the hall. 'Now to the river and the hospital regatta.'

Eleanor watched them go. 'She's very popular with the

gentlemen,' she said, wondering if she could ever learn to emulate her, and whether it would be worth the price if she did.

'So would you be if you had a wad of money and a ward to bestow on whoever took your fancy,' Doctor Marsham pointed out. 'Come on,' he added, starting down the corridor. 'You can watch me row – cheer on your fellow doctors.'

Eleanor tilted her chin. 'I will not,' she declared. 'They don't cheer me on.'

Doctor Marsham turned. 'It's no good declaring war on the army you want to join. Break into their ranks from the inside,' he said. For once there was little of his usual wry wit behind his words. 'Watch me – learn how to slip into their ranks without even being noticed.'

He gave her the merest hint of a smile. Eleanor felt her own mouth tighten. All right then, she thought. I shall.

***

There was a fresh breeze off the river that quite blew away Eleanor's cares. Afterwards, she thought, I shall worry about Sir Herbert and Daniel Bentley's foot, and Victoria too. But for now I shall simply enjoy myself. That was easy enough, as she and Doctor Marsham wended their way between the scattering of people who had come to watch. He had changed into shorts and a light-coloured blazer, and he was pushing Bessie, his bicycle.

The rest of the rowers were waiting for him, ready to launch his skiff for the singles race.

'Come on, Marsham,' one of them called. 'Get your idle bones down here before we're disqualified.' There was an edge to his tone.

Breaking in from the inside, are you, Doctor Marsham?

Eleanor wondered. He'd made no secret that his father was in trade, not the professions. It was just as well he hadn't forgotten – it seemed his fellow doctors were not going to.

'Damn,' he cursed. He pushed the bicycle at Eleanor. 'You made me late – you look after Bessie.' He ran towards the skiff. 'Don't forget to cheer!' he called over his shoulder as he boarded.

Eleanor found she was smiling as she pushed Bessie along. The machine was made of black iron and it smelled of oil and leather. She rather liked it.

The starting flag went down and the race began. Eleanor set off to follow the skiffs. At first, she paced them easily but as they got faster she found herself lagging a little. It was hard to see, too, because of the people lining the banks.

Someone pushed past her. 'Watch out, Doctor Bramwell!' It was Caslow, one of the other assistant doctors. He, unlike Eleanor, was sure he was destined for great things at the hospital. He turned and started walking backwards. 'Come on, Doctor,' he taunted. 'Ride the damned thing! Cheer him on.' He laughed derisively, then turned and trotted along the bank. 'Come on, Marsham!' he shouted. 'Come on, Marsham!'

Eleanor glanced at the river. The race was going to be close-fought, she thought. Well, if Caslow can shout and he doesn't even like Doctor Marsham, I certainly can. 'Come on, East London,' she called, somewhat tentatively. 'Come on, Marsham! Come on, the East London.'

She was getting left behind. It was the bicycle's fault – it was too heavy to push easily. She stared speculatively at Bessie, then carefully put one foot on the near pedal and scooted along. Faster.

'Come on, Marsham!'

Faster. The wind whipped her cheeks and tugged at her skirts. Faster.

'Come on, the East London.' People were beginning to stare. Eleanor smiled. 'Come on, Marsham. You can do it!' A woman tutted. Eleanor found she didn't care.

She bowled along to the finish line just in time to see Doctor Marsham's skiff cross it first. She clapped her hands in glee.

Caslow was holding his side with a stitch. He scowled at her. She smiled sweetly at him.

***

There was something wrong. Eleanor sensed it the moment she opened the front door, even before she heard the shouting from upstairs.

She went in and started to unpin her hat. Kate hurried forward to take it from her. Eleanor glanced into the drawing room. A pallid young man stood in front of the fireplace, examining his nails as if they were the most fascinating objects in the world.

'Who's that?' hissed Eleanor.

'Mr Neville, Lord Edward's secretary,' Kate whispered back. Before she could say any more the door of the guest room slammed.

Edward appeared at the top of the stairs. He leaned over the bannister.

'Robert!' he bellowed. 'Robert!' Eleanor's father came out of the drawing room just as Edward started downstairs. 'It's no use,' he said. 'She won't have me in the same room.'

'Perhaps if you spoke to her, rather than shouted at her,' Father suggested mildly, but the exasperation was plain on his face.

'What on earth have you done to her?' Eleanor asked, trying not to sound angry.

Edward made no such concession. 'I've ordered a carriage to take her to the country,' he said as he continued down. 'I've employed a nurse. I've engaged the best physician in London and...' Eleanor darted past him up the stairs, wondering how far she would get before one of them tried to stop her.

'Eleanor, don't you make it worse,' her father called.

'...she accuses me of cruelty!' Edward finished. He turned and jabbed a finger in the direction of the guest room. 'If that woman is not packed and ready in thirty minutes...' he screamed but did not specify what dreadful fate awaited her if she were not.

Eleanor did not dignify the outburst with a reply.

'Lord Edward,' said an unfamiliar voice at the bottom of the stairs.

'Neville!' Edward said. 'Welcome to Bedlam.'

Bedlam indeed, thought Eleanor, when she opened the bedroom door. Victoria was standing by the bed, hurling fistfuls of clothes onto the bed from her travel cases. Her face was pale and smeared with tears.

'He won't touch me!' she wailed when she saw Eleanor. 'I'll never let him touch me again!'

Eleanor crossed the room and grabbed her hands. 'Please,' she said. 'Calm down, do.'

Vicky wrenched free of her. 'Oh, Edward mustn't be connected with the slightest whiff of scandal,' she said. She went round to the other side of the bed. 'So I have to be bundled away in case I say anything.' She grabbed an armful of dresses and underthings and dumped them on the bed.

35

Eleanor took hold of her and forced her to turn round. 'Come, sit down,' she coaxed.

'I will not,' Victoria said. Her eyes were raw with crying and her hair was straggling free of its pins. She pushed Eleanor away from her and raced round to the other side of the bed. 'He says it isn't anything, this disease – that I'm just being silly.' She stared at her clothes – all the pretty things he had bought her since their marriage. 'Silly!' Vicky exclaimed. She threw a hairbrush out of the nearest case. 'No word of regret...' And then, as if she had thought of it now for the first time, she leaned forward on the case and whispered, 'What sort of woman would give him this disease?' Her face crumpled. 'What sort of dirty, slovenly, filthy...'

Eleanor strode over to her. 'A woman like you,' she said sharply. 'It respects no-one.'

Victoria turned and drew herself up to her full height. 'I've decided,' she declared loudly. 'I'm leaving him.'

'You don't mean it,' Eleanor said firmly. Vicky opened her mouth to shout a reply.

'Shhh!' Eleanor urged her. 'The servants will hear.'

'Good!' Vicky said even more loudly. 'Shall I tell them why the Chancellor's wife is being sent away from London?'

Again she pushed past Eleanor, who could only stare at her in despair. Before she could think of anything to say, the door opened.

'Sir Herbert!' Eleanor said, looking round. The best physician in London. She should have known.

'Good day, ladies.' He seemed vastly amused at Eleanor's obvious discomfiture. He laughed. 'Lady Carstairs, I was afraid I had a common washroom here...' he stooped and swept up something frilly from the floor and placed it on the bed, 'and not a lady's room.' He came a little way farther into the room, though he had not been invited. 'How are you?' he asked gently, and in that moment Eleanor could see how well his bedside manner would work – when he wanted it to.

Vicky brushed a strand of hair back from her forehead. 'Not well, Sir Herbert,' she murmured, like a sick child.

Sir Herbert laid his bag on a side table. 'So I've been told.' He opened the bag. 'Well, these little things are sent to try us.' He smiled at her, and again Eleanor marvelled at his sincerity. 'Now if you could just loosen your collar...' He pulled a stethoscope from the bag.

'I don't want to be examined,' Vicky said clutching at her throat.

'Now now, you're getting yourself into a tizzy, and there really is no need,' Sir Herbert said as he crossed the room to her. He glanced at Eleanor. 'And no need for you, either, Miss Bramwell.'

There was nothing Eleanor could say, but Vicky protested, 'I'd like Eleanor to stay.'

Eleanor looked from one to the other, unsure what to do for the best.

'No, no, Lady Carstairs,' Sir Herbert said. He ushered Eleanor out. 'No, no.'

Eleanor walked before him with all the dignity she could muster. She stopped to let him open the door for her and went out onto the landing.

Edward and Neville were there, talking quietly together. They looked over at her, then continued.

She went downstairs, thinking, Gentlemen, pray do

continue conspiring. Vicky might be a dizzy girl in many respects, but it seemed this once she was right about her husband's intentions.

***

Sir Herbert leaned back in the sofa in the drawing room and addressed his audience of Edward, Victoria, Eleanor and her father. 'Female hysteria,' he said. 'Overheated blood. Brought on by the long journey.' Eleanor glanced from him to Edward, who seemed eager enough to accept this new diagnosis, and then to her father, whose expression was carefully neutral. 'And', Sir Herbert added, 'disappointment over the pregnancy', he looked pointedly at Eleanor, 'and the unfortunate manner of telling her.' He paused, and the silence in the room grew uncomfortable. 'However,' he concluded, 'we are somewhat calmer now and have agreed to a compromise.'

'We shall live with my sister until our town house is ready,' Edward said. Victoria started to speak, but he cut her off. 'Victoria is perfectly amenable.'

'She barely knows Lady Peters,' Eleanor murmured.

As she expected, Edward ignored her. 'I'll wait until the carriage and the nurse arrive, but then I must attend to my duties,' he said. He started towards the door, which gave the signal for both Father and Sir Herbert to rise. Edward turned back at the open door. 'Meanwhile, I must be absolutely assured of confidentiality.'

'I've already given you my word,' Father said, sounding a smidgeon affronted. 'I'm very sorry about this, Edward.'

Edward nodded curtly, the briefest of acknowledgements.

Sir Herbert took his leave, promising to call on Victoria at Lady Peters' house. Edward followed him out of the room, and

Father shut the door on them.

'Poor Victoria,' Eleanor said. 'I can't believe she wants to stay with anyone from Edward's family.'

'It's none of your business what she wants,' Father said, as he crossed the room to take up his customary place in front of the fire.

Eleanor sighed. She might have known she would get little sympathy from him. 'You're right,' she said, wondering if any of the men who were so busy organizing Victoria's life had stopped to consider what she wanted. That was not the point though, at least not at the moment. She had embarrassed her father, and that had never been her intention. 'I'm sorry,' she said. Father said nothing, only stared at her gloomily. 'Whisky?' she asked after a moment, hoping to lighten the mood.

'Yes.'

Eleanor got up and went to the sideboard. She could feel him watching her as she poured the drinks.

'Good God,' he said. 'Here I am in the middle of the day, watching my daughter pour herself a large whisky and hardly turning a hair.' He paused. 'I must have failed you.'

Eleanor put down the decanter and turned, assuming it was a joke. 'No, you haven't,' she said; she saw, with some surprise, that he was serious and added, 'Really.'

'Your mother would have kept you under more control,' he said. His eyes were distant, as they often were when he thought of Mother. 'Softened you.'

Not if Lady Peters is right, Eleanor thought; but she didn't say it. She had hurt Father quite enough for one week.

Father took the glass from her. 'Medicine's a hard world,' he said. 'It's making you hard.' Is it? Eleanor wondered. She supposed that if it were, she would be the last to know. 'Perhaps you'd be better off out of it,' he said. He was almost pleading.

Eleanor could not look at him. Not that, she thought. Ask anything of me, Father, but that.

***

Eleanor leaned against the ward door and stared at Daniel Bentley as he tried to master his new crutch. He hopped and swung the crutch at the same time, managing to move forward all of some four inches, while a highly unappreciative Nurse Carr tried to support him.

'I shall have it in a minute,' he said to Eleanor and tried again, to no greater effect than before. Nurse Carr pulled a sour face.

'Use your crutch to lean on while you take a step with your good foot,' Eleanor said.

Daniel tried again, and again the result was a useless little rabbit hop that made his coarse hospital-issue nightshirt billow around him. 'I shall have it in a minute,' he repeated, and smiled at Eleanor with a mixture of bravado and embarrassment.

'Right, listen to me,' Eleanor said, deciding to take pity on the long-suffering Nurse Carr. She strode over to him. 'Lean on your crutch,' she said briskly. Daniel struggled to tuck the crutch under his arm. 'Go on then, lean on it.' Tentatively, Daniel put his weight on the crutch. 'Now, remain leaning on it and move the other foot a step.'

Daniel swung and hopped his usual few inches, only this time he almost overbalanced. 'I shall have it in a minute,' he said, as if it were the only phrase he knew.

'He's got to sort of swing, Doctor,' Nurse Carr said. She leaned forward and bellowed like a sergeant-major at Daniel, 'Swing your leg!'

Eleanor went to get a walking stick from the table.

'I'm not deaf,' Daniel said mildly. 'I shall have it in a minute,' he said to Eleanor as she came back.

'Watch,' Eleanor said. She hitched up her skirts with one hand and started to walk with the stick, singing one of her father's favourite music hall songs as she went: thump; step.

She stopped and looked at Daniel. He was watching her with a bemused expression. She went back to him. 'You have to do it with me.' She flashed him an encouraging smile and hitched up her skirts again.

They sang together, 'As I walk along the Bois de Boulogne', Daniel stumbled over the unfamiliar words and hopped along as he had before, 'with an independent air'. Hop. 'The ladies all declare', Daniel managed a tired, wobbly hop, 'there goes a millionaire.' He twisted round using the crutch as a support and managed to sit down just before he fell.

'Bleedin' useless.' Eleanor turned round to see who had spoken. It was John, the patient in the next bed. 'You should have taken mine off, Miss.'

'Not to worry,' Daniel said. 'I shall have it in a minute.'

Eleanor sat with him for a moment while he caught his breath, then helped him stand up. As she did so, she noticed Nurse Carr talking to Lady Peters just outside the ward.

Heaven only knew what she had made of the music hall song. With luck, she approved of them rather more than Nurse Carr had.

Eleanor helped Daniel into bed and attended to the few

other duties she was allowed, then left. As she went out into the corridor, Sir Herbert came round the corner, deep in conversation with Doctor Marsham, who was taking notes even as he walked. There was no avoiding them.

'Sir Herbert,' Eleanor said.

She dreaded his response, but he smiled jovially and said 'Aha! Our would-be surgeon.' His smile broadened, though Eleanor would not have thought that possible. 'How's the foot?'

'Very good, Sir.' And then, deciding it was time to rebuild her father's bridges if that were at all possible, 'Sir…'

But Sir Herbert interrupted, 'You know you've made a particular hit with Lady Peters. She thinks you're full of vitality.' He paused. 'Are you?' he added, somewhat archly.

Eleanor smiled, a trifle embarrassed. 'I hope so, Sir,' she said and then, because having braced herself to say something unpalatable she could not bear to leave it unsaid, 'Sir Herbert, I must thank you for your patience yesterday with Lady Carstairs.' She took a deep breath, wondering if it were possible to choke on mere words. 'I behaved very hastily and unwisely.'

In triumph, Sir Herbert was kindly, as he never was when she opposed him. 'Oh my dear,' he said. 'The young are ever trying to run before they can walk.' He lowered his voice to the confidential tone he might have used on a ward round. 'She'll be quite all right now.'

'I'm sure,' Eleanor said, though in truth she was no such thing. Sir Herbert started past her. She followed. 'I wonder, Sir Herbert, would you remember me to her?'

Sir Herbert walked quickly, and Eleanor had to hurry to keep up. 'Certainly,' he said. He turned back to Marsham, who was following more slowly. 'You'll be there, won't you,

Doctor Marsham?' Doctor Marsham looked up from his writing, clearly not following. 'Tuesday,' Sir Herbert explained. 'I need an anaesthetist.'

'An anaesthetist?' Eleanor asked but she already knew the answer.

'I can't do it without one,' he said. 'She's not a washerwoman, you know.' He laughed as though it were a great joke.

'Do what, Sir Herbert?' Doctor Marsham asked.

'An ovariectomy. The Chancellor's wife.'

'An ovari…' Eleanor stared at him in horror. 'Vicky?'

'Only thing for it,' Sir Herbert said. He stopped walking and turned to her. 'Whip out her ovaries.' He walked on, as if to forestall any further debate.

Eleanor hurried after him. 'But why?' she demanded. She glanced back at Doctor Marsham and saw that he was watching with interest. 'She has syphilis,' she hissed. 'What good…'

'She has a minor infection,' Sir Herbert said loudly, for Doctor Marsham's benefit. 'Brought on, no doubt, by the water abroad.'

Again, he walked away, and again Eleanor followed him. 'No!' she said. Let Doctor Marsham hear. Let the world hear, if it would save Vicky from this butcher's knife. 'You know she has syphilis.'

Sir Herbert whirled round. 'Don't be ridiculous,' he snapped. There were two spots of colour high on his cheeks. When he spoke again it was with forced quietness. 'Lady Carstairs is neurasthenic and hysterical – no more than that.' Eleanor stared at him, unable to decide which was worse: the thought that he might be so incompetent as to believe the nonsense he was spouting; or that he would put Vicky's health – perhaps her life – at risk in order to please Lord Edward. 'An ovariectomy will soon calm her down.'

He walked off again, and this time Eleanor let him go. Whatever he really believed, it was obvious there was no arguing with him.

I wish, she thought, I really wish I had not apologized to him.

Chapter 5

Eleanor brooded over the next few days, and nothing – not Father's songs nor Daniel Bentley's improvement on his crutches – could lighten her mood. The more she thought about what they were going to do to Vicky, the more devious it seemed, and the more angry she became.

Lady Peters was at home to visitors on Monday mornings. Eleanor got out her best coat and hat, very decorous in grey velvet with mother-of-pearl buttons, and went to see her.

When Eleanor was ushered into the drawing room, Lady Peters was attending to some correspondence. She did not stand when Eleanor entered. 'I'd let you see her with pleasure, but she's resting,' she said when she heard Eleanor's request, although she seemed to gain no great pleasure from Eleanor's visit. 'She's to have an operation tomorrow.' She peered at her letter through the lorgnette she was holding, and Eleanor realized it was a dismissal.

'I know,' she said, struggling to keep the impatience out of her voice. It seemed that however much Lady Peters had been taken by her, she had been more impressed with Sir Herbert. Well, Lady Peters might be a woman of fashion, but she did not seem totally narrow minded. 'Last week, Sir Herbert performed the same operation on a woman of twenty-four.'

Lady Peters put down the lorgnette. 'Yes?'

'She died,' Eleanor said flatly and watched the shock form on Lady Peters' face. 'An ovariectomy is a terrible thing.'

'Oh, come now,' protested Lady Peters. 'My brother may be self-centred but he'd never do anything terrible. And Sir Herbert…'

'Would say and do anything to remain in your good books.' She paused, wondering how far it would be necessary to go, and how far she would dare. 'And after all, you have a ward to bestow.'

Lady Peters put down the lorgnette. 'That's a bleak portrait of medical ethics.'

So, Eleanor thought, she was at least prepared to listen. 'They've brought her here,' she said, speaking quickly so that Lady Peters could not interrupt, 'where she sees no-one but you, to have the one operation which guarantees that she will never present Edward with a deformed child. How ethical is that?' she demanded. Before Lady Peters could say anything, she went on, 'It also means that his dazzling career can go from strength to strength.' The more she spoke, the angrier she became, but before she could bring her argument to a conclusion, the drawing room doors opened.

She turned. Victoria was standing there. She was wan, with dark shadows around her eyes, and her ivory coloured house-dress only served to make her seem more wraith-like. Eleanor's heart went out to her.

'I thought I heard you, Eleanor,' she said. 'No-one told me.' Her hand trembled, and with the other she kept hold of the door frame as she spoke.

Eleanor turned back to Lady Peters. You see, she thought,

you see what you have helped do to her?

Lady Peters pursed her lips. After a moment she seemed to come to a decision. She put her letters aside and stood up. 'Don't overtire her,' she commanded and swept out, barely acknowledging Eleanor's reply.

'Vicky, what's this about an operation?' Eleanor asked once they were alone and the door was closed.

'Sir Herbert says the infection is nothing,' Vicky said. She stood in the doorway, twisting her handkerchief in her hands. 'And he says that hysteria has weakened my heart.' She sounded desperate and defensive.

'Even if that were true, it's no reason to remove your ovaries,' Eleanor said.

But Vicky went on, 'And that you've upset me over nothing.' She walked towards Eleanor, who saw that she was near tears. Perhaps because of that, she turned and stood facing away.

Eleanor wanted to be kind, to comfort her. But where would comfort get Vicky now? A place on Sir Herbert's operating table and then on the mortuary slab. 'Vicky, don't let them lie to you,' she said. What, she wondered desperately, would convince her? 'They're giving you mercury, aren't they?' Vicky turned to look at her. Her skin was so pale it was almost translucent. 'Mercury is a treatment for syphilis,' Eleanor went on, determined to spare Vicky nothing, if doing so would only save her life. 'And whatever they've told you about the ovariectomy…'

'The operation is very popular, they say,' Vicky said. She sat down and stared at her hands, not at Eleanor. 'All manner of women are having it.'

'All manner of women are dying from it!' Eleanor

47

exploded, her patience finally at an end.

'How do you know?' demanded Vicky, finally looking at Eleanor. 'You're not even a surgeon,' she added, looking away; but her voice was quavering.

'It's a stupid and dangerous fashion.'

'I don't believe you!' There were tears on Vicky's cheeks.

How many more times would she make her friend cry, Eleanor wondered? She sat down and said quietly, 'You know I wouldn't lie to you.'

'Stop it!' Vicky shouted. 'Stop it, I don't want to hear.' She twisted round and sobbed into the chair.

Eleanor stared at her for a moment, and then, furious and despairing at once, turned and marched out. Lady Peters was in the hallway, arranging flowers. She turned, with a tiger lily still in her hand, and stared at Eleanor as she stalked past.

Not overtire Vicky? Eleanor thought as she went out into the street. Not upset her? It was the lies of Sir Herbert that should be upsetting, not the truth.

She really should have gone home before she went to the East London for the afternoon but she could not bear to face her father, who would, no doubt, take her to task for visiting Lady Peters at all. Instead she found her feet taking her to the riverside. The summer air was heavy with the scent of new-mown grass, and the sun was warm on her face. Yet not even that could dispel her fury. There were only a few people about, taking the air or reading on the benches; but Doctor Marsham was rowing a skiff on the water. She watched him for a moment, wishing she could join him, perhaps work off her anger in good wholesome exercise. That was not an option open to her, and so she did the most a gentlewoman might and strode along as fast as her skirts and her corset would allow.

She came at last to the boathouse. Bessie was propped up against the door. Eleanor almost went past, but then she stopped. It was a mad idea, a dangerous idea, a reputation-wrecking idea. She liked it all the better for that.

She looked round. There was no-one in sight. Before she had time for second thoughts, she went inside and hitched up her skirts with one hand, while with the other she held the bicycle upright. Then she clambered onto the saddle and pushed herself off with both feet. The bicycle wobbled.

Feet on the pedals, she thought, and managed it at the second or third attempt. She pushed round and down, down and round – and found that she was bowling along. Strangely, the faster she went the more stable the bicycle seemed to be. The wind whipped her face and threatened her hat. She found she was smiling for the first time that day. She glanced down and saw a flash of lacy, white underwear.

Oh dear, she thought; but she didn't stop. She went right past a nanny and her charges, and a gentleman who tutted at her, but they didn't matter nearly so much as the wind on her face.

At last, she thought she had better take Bessie back. Reluctantly, she returned to the boathouse, only to find Doctor Marsham waiting for her. It was only when she started to slow down that she realized that she didn't know how to stop.

Fortunately, Doctor Marsham ran up to her and grabbed the handlebars. 'Oh,' she gasped. 'Mr Marsham!' She sat for a moment, quite breathless. 'How much would one of these things cost?'

'Your reputation,' he said, with his usual dourness. 'Give it here, Miss Bramwell.'

Eleanor swung her leg over the saddle, carefully disentangling her skirts. 'And what about your reputation?' she asked. 'If you're not careful, you'll be known as a fast young man'. She smiled at Doctor Marsham's obvious bemusement and walked off.

By the time she reached the hospital, she was in a much better mood, having managed to turn her thoughts away from Vicky and towards Daniel Bentley.

She put on her apron and went to the ward. She fetched Daniel's notes, but as she approached his bed Nurse Carr intercepted her.

'I'm sorry, Doctor,' she said stiffly.

'Yes, Nurse?' Eleanor said, not quite understanding.

'Sir Herbert's left instructions,' Nurse Carr said, as if that explained everything.

'But I must see my patient.'

Nurse Carr took the notes from Eleanor's hand. 'Mr Bentley is under Sir Herbert again,' she said.

'But why?' Eleanor demanded. 'His foot?' If it had gone gangrenous as Sir Herbert seemed to think it had it would need radical surgery; perhaps Sir Herbert assumed she would oppose it. It was nonsense – she had never been against surgery where there was a genuine need for it – but she could see how he might think it.

Nurse Carr's face softened. 'His foot's doing very well, Doctor,' she said. 'Healing nicely – and he's doing better on his crutches. Eleanor started forward. Again, Nurse Carr barred the way. 'I'm sorry,' she said softly. 'I wish I could let you in, but I can't.'

Eleanor stared at her, appalled. Then, realizing that there

was no point arguing with her, she turned and left. She walked the corridors furiously until she spotted Sir Herbert.

She hurried after him and demanded, 'Why have you banned me from your wards?'

'You are banned from the entire hospital,' he said, without a trace of anger.

'Why?' she said, wishing it sounded less like a wail. 'What have I done?'

Sir Herbert pulled out his pocket watch and glanced at it. 'Do you know where I should be at this very minute?' Eleanor shook her head. 'Operating on Lady Carstairs.' Now he was unable to keep the irritation out of his voice. He walked off down the corridor. Eleanor followed. 'Thanks to you, she has decided to do without.'

'I thought she was going ahead with it,' she said, for her part unable to suppress her delight at the decision.

'So did we,' snapped Sir Herbert. He stopped and glared at Eleanor. 'Instead, wherever you go – tears and tantrums.'

'I merely explained...' Eleanor protested.

Sir Herbert marched off again. 'You tried to explain matters that you had no business even discussing,' he said. 'She's not even your patient.' There was some truth in that, Eleanor supposed; but if Sir Herbert had been more honest with Vicky, Eleanor would have had no need to talk to her. She opened her mouth to say as much, but Sir Herbert went on, 'You're totally inexperienced in treating this condition.'

'I'm a qualified physician,' Eleanor said. 'I know about venereal disease.'

'If you are a lady you should be ashamed even to say those

words.' Disgust replaced fury on Sir Herbert's face. 'You lack delicacy, tact…'

'Hypocrisy!' Eleanor said, struggling to keep her voice below a shout. 'Deceit.'

'This profession has no room for rampaging females with grand ideas,' Sir Herbert said, with all the finality of a judge handing down a death sentence. 'Medicine is as much to do with politics and diplomacy as with the study of disease.'

Eleanor felt herself flush with anger. He stood there, inflating his reputation at the expense of his patients' health – their livelihoods, their very lives – and he had the barefaced cheek to call her indelicate. In that moment she decided she hated him, from the top of his gingery head to the tips of his well-polished boots. 'No!' she shouted. 'Medicine has nothing to do with politics. Only a corrupt charlatan would say it has.' She was breathless with rage and her nails bit into her palms where she was clenching her fists.

'You are no longer welcome in this hospital!' Sir Herbert thundered and stormed off down the corridor.

Eleanor pursued him. There was no time for delicacy, no point in tact. 'A charlatan who butchers his patients for fat fees and to bolster his own pathetic reputation,' she shouted, not caring who might hear.

Sir Herbert turned, blue eyes bulging out of his red face with the force of his fury. 'Get out before I have you thrown out,' he bellowed.

Eleanor stood her ground. 'I will not,' she shouted, incandescent with rage now. 'I'll talk to the governors.'

She knew she had made a mistake. Sir Herbert drew himself up. He smiled slyly. 'Oh, the governors are in complete agreement with me,' he said in a more normal tone of voice. 'You are no longer to be allowed on the wards at any time.' Eleanor stared at him, trying to make sense of what he had just said. He had taken her life away from her. Didn't he realize that? As always, he was expansive in victory. 'The female brain, being smaller and weaker,' he pontificated, 'is not suited to scientific matters.' He smiled at her in an almost kindly fashion – as he might have, she thought, at a small child who had wandered from its nursery and, uninvited, entered the drawing room. 'God made women for other things than medicine. Go home to your father,' he said and started to walk away. Just as Eleanor thought she was free of him, he turned and came back. 'And find yourself a husband.' He touched her on the shoulder in a way she found altogether too familiar. And then, at last, he left her.

She stood for a moment, trying to compose herself. Banned. Banned from the hospital, from the wards. It was more than she knew how to cope with.

Somehow, she found herself outside in the bright sunshine, still in her apron and with her coat in her hands. She marched across the courtyard, cheeks flaming, sure that everyone there – gentlemen and women, working folk come to the hospital for help, doctors on their way to and from their duties, everyone in the whole world – was watching her.

Banned. Banned for speaking the truth. The more the words rang in her brain, the faster she walked, and not even the thought that Vicky had not gone ahead with the operation could calm her.

She could be sure Daniel Bentley would have his operation. Who would there be, in that hospital full of charlatans, to tell him not to let Sir Herbert take off his foot?

'I'm sorry,' said a voice behind her. She kept walking. Doctor Marsham came round in front of her, forcing her to stop. 'They're arrogant fools. The whole damned place is so choked with arrogance.' He stopped and stared at her. She wondered if he could see that she was almost in tears. 'Sir Herbert is being very unfair.'

'If you won't tell him, don't tell me,' she said, her voice so unsteady that now he must know. She marched off, forcing him to run to keep up.

'How can I?' he asked. 'I need the job.'

'So do I, but that doesn't matter, does it?' Eleanor snapped. She knew he meant he needed the money, which in truth she didn't, but she needed the job for the sake of her spirit, and who was to say that was less important? 'A woman doesn't belong in your world, in your wards, on your bicycles.' She was crying now, and she couldn't bear to let him see it. She stumbled away. 'Oh go away, Mr Marsham,' she said as she went, trying not to notice the hurt on his face.

***

Eleanor paced up and down her father's consulting room. She had walked off her anger, if not her despair. 'I'd do the same again,' she said defiantly. Her father sat at his bench, where he had been working at his microscope. The early afternoon sun shafting in at the window gilded the brass, and turned his white hair almost silver. 'The very idea of an ovariectomy,' she said, expecting him to protest.

'Quite,' he said. She raised her eyebrows at him. 'I'm not a barbarian, Eleanor. I don't agree with hacking into bodies willy-nilly.' She had forgotten, she supposed. He had been so angry with her for talking to Vicky in the first place that, in her mind, she had lumped him in with Edward and Sir Herbert. 'I'm very pleased that Victoria refused.'

'And how will you feel tomorrow if this becomes public?' she asked.

'Well,' he said, 'I hope it doesn't. But if so, a life is rather more important than a politician's career.'

'Or mine,' Eleanor said bitterly, though she knew he was right.

Father stood up. 'I think maybe it's time you began to accept that you have no future at the East London.' He crossed over to his desk. He started to make a note in his journal. 'You'll have to be satisfied with private practice.'

'Oh no you don't!' Eleanor said, only half laughing.

'I know it's hard, but you can always come in with me,' Father said. He tried a smile. 'Perhaps then Kate, I and the whole damned household can get rid of these headlice.'

'Father don't make a joke of it,' Eleanor said fiercely. 'I want to work where I'm needed.'

'This is where you're needed,' he said sombrely. Eleanor refused to answer, and Father continued writing. When he spoke again, the old mischievous glint was back in his eye. 'Besides, if you take some private patients, perhaps we'll see a financial return for your training.' He walked over to his bureau.

'I'd rather be a governess,' she said, and when he didn't answer immediately, she added defiantly, 'I could!'

'You could also be a cleaner on the trams, but it seems a bit drastic,' he said. Eleanor made a sour face at him. He picked up a pile of notes. 'Look,' he said, offering them to her, 'some ladies who might just accept a female doctor.'

'Nothing too complicated, I hope?' Eleanor asked sourly,

without taking them. 'Ingrown toe-nails, the occasional hot flush.' And she thought, but did not add aloud, things my smaller, weaker, unsuitable female brain can manage.

'Darling,' Father said, 'life's going to be difficult enough just being a doctor without looking for hopeless battles to fight all the time.' Eleanor glared at him. They weren't his battles, and he hadn't had to put up with Sir Herbert's condescension. But then he went on, more gently, 'It makes me exhausted just watching you.' He proffered the pile of notes again. 'Now, indulge an old man?' Eleanor took them, reluctantly. She tried to force a smile but didn't succeed. 'I guarantee, there's not one hyperchondriac amongst them,' Father said and went back to his workbench.

Eleanor sighed and hoped Father would not hear. She took the notes and went and sat in the garden, where the scent of rhododendrons pleased but could not soothe her. She leafed through Father's notes disconsolately. Fainting fits. Anaemia. Nothing much more difficult than that to tax her female brain.

She slapped the papers together and stood up, thinking that perhaps a cup of tea would help her find a way out of her predicament. She started down the path towards the house, only to see Victoria coming towards her.

'Eleanor,' she called. She had regained something of her old vitality and had dressed with care in a fawn skirt and high-necked blouse, and a neat, feathered hat. 'I insisted that Edward brought me,' she said and clasped Eleanor's hands. Eleanor looked round and saw Edward standing near the French doors. His face was set like stone. Vicky sat down on the bench. Eleanor joined her. 'So!' Vicky said, as if it answered any and all questions.

'How are you?' Eleanor asked, not trusting the brightness in her friend's voice, but not wishing to distress her again.

'How do I look?' Vicky asked, showing Eleanor her profile.

'You look well,' Eleanor said carefully. It was true. There was colour in her cheeks, and the dark rings were gone from round her eyes. And yet...Eleanor thought.

'I am,' declared Vicky. 'Edward is as attentive as ever, and I am a perfectly composed lady.' Eleanor stared at her, not quite believing her. Vicky matched her gaze for a moment, then looked away. 'Well,' she admitted, 'not perfectly, perhaps.' She stared at her hands. 'But composed enough to realize how fortunate I am to have a friend like you.'

Eleanor glanced at Edward. He hadn't moved. 'Edward has accepted that you won't have the operation?' she asked.

'Yes,' Vicky said. She smiled. 'And I have accepted that some silly little infection is neither here nor there between man and wife.' Eleanor suppressed a sigh. She ought to argue about it, but she was tired of arguing, tired of being in the wrong, tired of bearing the weight of her father's disapproval. That, most of all. She might have gathered her courage and changed her mind but Vicky went on, 'A silly little infection, probably from the water on the continent.' She stared straight at Eleanor, who thought, she does know. She does. 'But', Vicky continued, 'we have decided not to have a child for a few years, anyway – just to be safe.'

What does it matter what they say it is, just as long as the infection is being treated properly, Eleanor thought. 'There's time, yet,' she agreed cautiously.

'Yes,' Vicky said. 'And men will be men.' She laughed, but Eleanor thought, yes – and women will suffer for it; but she could not bear to spoil what happiness Victoria had managed to achieve. So when Vicky said, 'See how grown up I am? All's well that ends well,' she merely returned her smile.

***

The next two days passed slowly. No patients came to see Eleanor, and without the hospital to visit, she had nothing to occupy her time except reading. When she had exhausted the *British Medical Journal* and the *Journal of Physiology* she turned to the women's journals that she usually despised. It was in one of those that she saw the item of apparel that so scandalized Kate.

All that was required was a little surgery on one of Eleanor's least favourite skirts. A few minutes with the scissors and a quick bit of embroidery, and the skirt had become a pair of ladies' trousers. When it was done, she stood in front of the mirror in the drawing room admiring her handiwork, while Kate crouched on the floor gathering the hems of the trouser legs.

'There,' Eleanor said triumphantly. 'All I need now is the bicycle.' She bent her knee to show off the trousers. 'What do you think?'

Kate looked a bit disapproving but was saved from having to say anything by the ringing of the doorbell. 'Be one of your father's patients, Miss.' She scurried off. 'I won't be a minute.'

Eleanor admired herself in the mirror. No doubt the gathers could have been more even, and the unevenness of the hems might want disguising – tuck them into my boots, she thought; but on the whole it wasn't a bad job.

'Miss Bramwell ain't seeing anyone,' she heard Kate say.

'Nonsense,' said Lady Peters briskly. 'It's ten o'clock. She's not ill.' There was a rustle of silks. 'I'll wait in here.' She breezed into the room like a small black galleon under full sail.

58

'Lady Peters!' Eleanor exclaimed.

Lady Peters took up a position in the centre of the room. 'With a substantial sum of money to bestow and a world full of needs, you would think, wouldn't you, that there would be some way of bringing the two together?' She brought her hands together in demonstration. The feathers on her hat bobbed.

Eleanor stared at her in bewilderment. 'Would you like a cup of tea?' she asked, hoping it would slow down Lady Peters long enough for her to start making sense.

Lady Peters dismissed the suggestion with a wave of her hand. Without waiting to be asked, she sat down on the sofa. 'I know and you know that a woman like me is a red rag to a bull to a woman like you.' She scowled. 'And Sir Herbert is no better.'

Eleanor struggled to follow this pronouncement. Deciding she had failed, she said, 'I'm sorry?'

'He sees me only as some silly creature to be humoured, courted…flirted with. Thinks I understand nothing.' She stared hard at Eleanor. 'As you do.' Eleanor hadn't really stopped to consider it before. Now that she did, she supposed it was true. She thought Lady Peters was a kind of grown-up version of Vicky: kind-hearted and good fun but flighty and without a thought in her head except the latest scandal and the newest fashion. The only thing that really surprised her was that Lady Peters might have registered her thoughts when she herself had not. 'I believe you are not attending the hospital any more?' Eleanor looked away, not wishing to open the subject for discussion. Lady Peters went on, 'And I am sorry that your Mr Bentley lost his foot.'

Eleanor's jaw clenched. 'His foot, his job, his pride.'

She spat out the words. 'I'm not the only one Sir Herbert wreaked his damned spite on.' Lady Peters looked taken aback. 'I'm sorry,' Eleanor said; but she meant it only for swearing, not for the thought behind it.

But Lady Peters laughed aloud. 'Trousers', she said, pointing at Eleanor's legs, 'and oaths. Maybe you're more of a match for the gentlemen than they realize.' She gestured to a chair, as if she were the hostess and Eleanor the guest. When Eleanor was seated, she said, 'Now, I have a proposition to put to you...'

Eleanor listened and when she had heard it all, she smiled for the first time since the trouble with Victoria had begun.

Chapter 6

Lady Peters' proposition was to turn the property in Thrift Street into an infirmary, with Eleanor as its physician.

'Madness,' Father said when they told him. 'Sheer madness.' But he did not seriously oppose them.

***

Two weeks later, Eleanor took him to see what they had done. They left their carriage on the main road with instructions to wait and picked their way through an ever-narrowing maze of side-streets and alleys. The cobbles were slick with mud and excrement, and a ghosting of fog hung in the air. The rhythmic pounding of a far-off blacksmith's hammer counterpointed the rumble of the steam trains and the shrill cries of the pigs and calves waiting for the butcher's knife in an abattoir somewhere nearby. And everywhere there were smells: the stink of urine and hot metal from the smith's forge, charcoal and coal as well as stale, burned meat. Eleanor noticed none of it as she led her father deeper into the labyrinth.

They turned a corner and emerged across the way from Thrift Street. Eleanor stared proudly at the building.

'It's a slum,' her father said. He gazed around him. 'A slum in a slum.'

For a moment, Eleanor saw it with his eyes: the soot-grimed walls and windows, the washing strung above the street from one tenement window to another, the wailing of an underfed child carried by a woman hurrying by.

'Tenements, abattoirs, brothels,' Father went on. Eleanor pulled away and went towards the Thrift Street Infirmary, as they had decided to call it. 'This whole area is the haunt of criminals – the scum of the city.' He hung back. A couple of urchins, filthy and gaunt-faced, eyed him from a doorway opposite.

Eleanor turned back. 'Well, I shouldn't stand there long, Father,' she teased, 'in case they all jump you.' She went in.

Lady Peters was already in the infirmary, along with Nurse Carr, whom they had lured away from the East London. Father joined them a moment later, in the waiting room. His expression softened when he saw her; it didn't hurt, Eleanor thought, that Nurse Carr had done so much to clean the place out. The floor was scrubbed, the bare brick walls clean. Dust motes danced in the morning light.

'Six beds,' she said and led them through a side room to show them the ward, 'Kitchen.' She pointed at another smaller room, 'Bathroom.' She came out into the ward, a long room made to seem longer by the white walls that picked up the sunlight shafting through the high windows. She pointed across it to a smaller room off to the side. 'And a consulting room.' She couldn't keep the wonder out of her voice. Her consulting room, from where nobody – neither Sir Herbert nor anyone else – could ban her. 'We'll be open for general consultation between ten and twelve. Those that need admitting…'

'But not surgical cases?' protested Father.

'Oh yes,' Eleanor said. 'We'll take surgical patients

eventually.' She strode off to the other end of the room, past a piano that sat there somewhat incongruously.

'Eleanor! For goodness' sake, you've only ever assisted,' Father said.

'I'm not the only doctor in London,' retorted Eleanor more tartly than she had intended. She turned back at him and smiled, to soften it. She was quite sure he knew that she intended to do at least some surgery herself.

'I'm sure we'll find expertise when we need it,' Lady Peters said. She went to join Eleanor. 'There's never a shortage of men,' she said with an arch smile as she went past Father.

'A woman daring to run an infirmary,' he said; but Eleanor could see he was resigned to it. 'You'll be ridiculed. Scorned.'

He was right, he was right, Eleanor thought. She wandered back through the ward, marvelling at it. 'Let them scorn me all they like,' she said. 'I really don't care.' Nurse Carr was sweeping the floor and her broom sent up a cloud of dust. Lady Peters tried out a scale on the piano. There was nothing extraordinary about either thing – except that they were happening in her infirmary. Hers and Lady Peters', anyway.

'You'll be packed out with scamps and paupers,' Father said; and then, mournfully, 'Scabies. Nits.'

Eleanor stopped by the fireplace to examine the stove.

'From my bridge partner,' Lady Peters said, behind her. Eleanor turned. Father was standing by the piano. 'We asked for five pounds and she gave us this instead,' Lady Peters said with a voice full of mock affront. She chuckled.

Father picked out a scale, rather more smoothly than Lady Peters had. Then he pulled up a stool and started to play 'When You Were Sweet Sixteen', one of his favourite music hall songs.

Eleanor rested against the wall to listen to her father sing. He never would play without singing.

'I love you as I never loved before,' he sang, 'since first I met you on the village green. Come to me or my dream of love is o'er' and his voice near broke with the tragedy of it. Nurse Carr rolled her eyes at Eleanor who smiled back at her. Lady Peters smiled girlishly at him. 'I love you as I loved you,' he sang; and she joined him for the chorus 'When you were sweet, when you were sweet sixteen.'

Eleanor wandered off through the infirmary: ward, waiting room, kitchen…

'Again,' Lady Peters cried. 'Again!' And Father struck up the tune again.

…Consulting room.

Behind her, they began to sing the song again. And as Eleanor surveyed her new world, she smiled.

***

The Thrift Street Infirmary was not properly open when its first patient arrived. Eleanor and Nurse Carr had just finished checking the drugs and the bandages, and Daniel Bentley – whom Lady Peters had employed as a porter and general factotum – had brought in the coal ready for the official opening the next morning. The street door was flung open and a large, florid-faced man staggered in, leaning on the shoulder of a much smaller one. He saw Eleanor and screamed something incoherent.

'Doctor?' the smaller man asked, looking straight past Eleanor. The larger man screamed again and they both staggered forward.

'We're not open yet,' Daniel said and moved to bar their

way as fast as his crutches would allow.

'Doctors!' snarled the fat man. 'I hate the bastards!'

'We was having a drink; then this,' the smaller man explained as he helped him sit. 'Well, he sicked up first.'

Nurse Carr pulled a face and hurried off to get a bowl.

'Shut the door, Mr Bentley,' Eleanor called. She turned to the thin man. 'What's his name?' They both stank of cheap gin and unwashed bodies, and the fat man's jacket was stained yellow with vomit.

'Undertakers,' the fat man said as if in reply. 'Give us an honest undertaker any day.'

'Me name's Paul Gardner,' he said. Eleanor looked at him in exasperation. 'He's Frank Harrison, Miss,' he said, while the other man rambled on to himself. 'Screaming with pain,' Paul added. 'I thought he was going to die. Well, he was holding his…' he hesitated.

'What?' demanded Eleanor.

'Well, holding his…belly, Miss.' Nurse Carr arrived with the bowl and pushed him unceremoniously out of the way. 'If there's a doctor, Miss…' he said.

'I'm a doctor,' Eleanor said and moved in to start the examination. She had no more than touched Frank Harrison's abdomen when he flung his arms up with a scream of rage. He knocked Nurse Carr, and the bowl flew out of her hands and clattered on the floor.

Eleanor stared at it for a moment. The scum of the city, Father had said. They were all watching her, seeing how she would react, whether she could deal with him. She licked her lips and moved in again.

'Get your hands off me,' he bellowed. He whipped a

gin bottle out of the pocket of his greatcoat and brandished it at them like a knife. He walked forwards slowly, with the bottle outstretched. Eleanor backed away. So did the others.

'Here,' Daniel shouted. 'You can't do that to her!' He yanked at Harrison's arm, but the big man simply kicked his crutch out from under him.

Frank smashed the bottle on the edge of the table. Shards of glass flew everywhere and the broken end in his hand glinted wickedly in the light.

He darted at Nurse Carr, who dodged back. 'You'll be up before the magistrates,' she said weakly.

'Oi, you can pack that in straight away,' Paul said.

Frank whirled. He lunged at Paul, who skipped out of his way. 'All right,' yelled Frank. 'Come on, you bastard!' He slashed at Paul, who jerked his head back at the last minute.

'Want me to fetch your Polly?' Paul shouted. 'Do you?' Frank hesitated. 'I will,' Paul threatened. 'She'll sort you.'

Frank hurled himself at Paul, who dived out of the way. Frank slammed into the wall and then grabbed his side. His lips skinned back from his teeth and he let out a moan.

There was a moment of calm in which Nurse Carr helped Daniel to his feet. Eleanor looked at them all, suddenly understanding that she – not Daniel, not Nurse Carr – had to deal with this, or she would indeed, as her father had said, be packed out with scamps and rogues.

She took a deep breath, and in her most imperious voice said, 'I think we've had enough of this sort of behaviour.' She took a step towards Frank. He jabbed the bottle at her. 'Put that bottle down,' she commanded, and held out her hand for it.

'Watch him, Miss,' Daniel called out. 'He's a mad sod.'

Frank drew the bottle back, as if preparing to hit her with it. He winced, then looked down at his free arm in puzzlement.

'You're very drunk and very foolish,' she said, as if she were scolding a small child.

In answer, Frank began to cry. He held out his hand. Blood poured from a long gash in his forearm. 'You've hurt us now,' he wailed.

Eleanor took the bottle from him. 'Water, sutures and lint, please, Nurse Carr,' she said crisply. She handed the bottle to Daniel and put her arm round Frank. Together, she and Paul managed to get him to the consulting room.

Eleanor gave Frank a dose of morphine and sutured his arm. He blasphemed till she was almost done and then sobered up abruptly. Then she put his arm in a sling. She had decided that, whatever the problem with his abdomen, now was not the time to insist on an examination, as it would probably harm more than help him. No doubt he would be back if the pain persisted.

'I'm sorry, Miss,' he said, touching his disreputable old bowler as Daniel saw him to the street door. 'Always disgusting drunk.' Eleanor could only agree but hoped it didn't show. 'I'm sorry, Miss,' he repeated as Daniel chivvied him out of the room.

Daniel opened the door for him with his free hand. He pushed his face close to Frank's. 'And don't bother coming back,' he said.

As soon as he had gone, Eleanor let out a huge sigh. 'Meek as a lamb!' she said. She could not keep the exultation out of her voice. 'My first difficult patient, and he was no problem at all.' Nurse Carr smoothed down her bloodied apron but kept her own counsel. Eleanor refused to allow her spirits to be dampened. 'Well,' she said. 'Onward.' She picked up her clipboard from the top of the piano. Much had been done, but much still remained to do if they were to open on time in the morning, and she did not expect to get home before dark. 'My colleagues may not like a lady doctor, but the patients don't seem to mind one little bit.'

***

Lady Cora arrived without warning the next morning, while Eleanor and her father were still at breakfast. She seated herself opposite Eleanor, who was tucking into her devilled kidneys and scrambled eggs. Her father was helping himself from the buffet on the sideboard; he had been late down to breakfast, which was unusual for him.

'We must impress upon the Bishop that the Thrift is, first and foremost, a Christian undertaking,' Lady Peters said. She was dressed in her usual black dress, but this time she had added a froth of mauve lace at her throat and sported a hat decorated with feathers and net.

'Well, so we are,' Eleanor said, scooping up a forkful of egg and wishing she could turn the conversation to yesterday's small triumph. She hadn't even had a chance to tell Father yet.

'If he's going to fund an anaesthetist, we have to convince him that we serve only honest, deserving people.'

Father turned round. Eleanor saw, to her surprise, that he was holding only a coffee cup. He usually made a good breakfast. 'How do you assess a man's honesty before you start mending his bones?'

'It's simple enough,' Eleanor said dismissively. She waved her hand, ignoring the fact that she was still holding her fork.

'Church-going, sober, respectable people.' Well, she thought, Frank Harrison had been neither sober nor respectable, but he hadn't said he didn't go to Church. Probably just as well she hadn't asked him. She decided that, on second thoughts, it was probably better not to tell Father and Lady Peters about him.

Father scowled. 'You don't realize what this infirmary of yours entails.' He came and sat down at the table.

'I know it's desperately needed,' Lady Cora said, 'and that's enough for me.'

'High-falutin' ideas about the deserving poor,' Father muttered. He stared sourly at his plate. 'The poor are foul and bad tempered and drunk.' Kate started to take the plate away but he snatched it back. 'And why shouldn't they be?' Eleanor raised her eyebrows at Lady Peters, who smiled back sardonically. It was fairly clear what Father had been up to without Eleanor to keep an eye on him. He looked from one to the other. 'And what has temperance to do with health?' he demanded abruptly.

'A great deal, I should have thought,' Lady Peters said tartly. 'Late night?'

'Father,' Eleanor said to change the subject, 'the Church is very welcome, and when the Bishop knows he'll be funding life-saving operations…'

'You've never done an operation in your life,' Father cut in. Before Eleanor could protest, he went on, 'When I was a young sawbones among the Zulus, we had no anaesthetic.' He sipped his coffee. Eleanor rolled her eyes. She had heard this one many times, even if Lady Peters had not – though by her expression, she had. 'A swig of whisky and tied to the table. Arms off. Legs off.' He put the cup down with a clatter. 'No nonsense.'

Lady Peters chuckled. 'You're a sweet old, hard old pirate.' She got up and went round the table. 'And we don't believe a word you say.' She patted him on the cheek. He was visibly charmed and stood as Kate saw her out.

Eleanor watched her go. 'What an enthusiast she's turned out to be,' she said. She smiled, remembering how she had dismissed Lady Peters when they first met; besides, anyone who could get round her father that easily was not to be trifled with.

Father sat back down again at the table. Eleanor got up to go, taking half a slice of toast with her. 'And what a grump you are,' she said, genially.

Just as she got to the door, Father said, 'Your first patient arrives at two o'clock.' Eleanor turned and stared at him in surprise. It was the first she'd heard of it. 'Don't be late home again,' he warned.

'A private patient? Who?'

'Peggy Heart,' Father said, as if no further explanation were needed. When Eleanor didn't react, he went on, 'Miss Peggy Heart.' Eleanor stared at him in bewilderment. '*The* Miss Peggy Heart.' She had it then – Peggy Heart was a music hall singer. It was no wonder Father expected she would have heard of the woman. She nodded. 'And treat her gently,' he warned. 'She's not one of your ruffians.'

'How did she hear about me?' Eleanor asked, round a mouthful of toast.

'It's what we agreed,' Father pointed out. 'New female patients to you.' He cheered up visibly. 'Your first five bob.'

Eleanor considered. 'Not much.' She took another bite of toast. 'But it's a start.' Father stared at her as if he had a few more things to say on the subject, if only he could summon the energy. 'It'll be good to start paying my way.'

'At last!' Father said, with something of his more usual mischief. He raised his eyes to Heaven. 'Her education pays fruit!'

'And as my private practice grows, it can support my work at the Thrift,' she said, enjoying the expression of mock dismay on Father's face. 'The work that really matters,' she added. She left the room and shut the door firmly before he could protest.

***

When Eleanor got to the Thrift, she was delighted to find the waiting room packed with patients. True, many of them were filthy, and they lent the place a certain odour of unwashed hair and bodies.

Her first morning at the Thrift passed quickly enough – she saw several cases of dropsy, lanced a gumboil and confirmed a pregnancy. Then Frank Harrison came in. Thankfully, this time he was sober, and though he still reeked of gin, his suit had been cleaned off a bit. He stretched his arm out in front of him pathetically, but with the other he clutched his abdomen.

Eleanor took him over to a table, and Nurse Carr stripped the bandage off his arm. The wound had bled through the sutures, so Eleanor cleaned it again with lysol.

While she was dabbing it he said, 'I just need something to ease the pain, Miss.' His face was beetroot red and he was sweating profusely. 'That stuff you gave me yesterday – that worked a treat.'

'Morphine?' Eleanor asked. 'I gave you that while we stitched your arm.' She wiped away the last of the blood. 'It's not something we give just because the patient decides he needs it.' Frank took a long, shuddering breath. For an awful moment, Eleanor thought he might beg. She stopped working on his arm. 'Mr Harrison, the pain is not from your arm, and well you know it.' He bit his lip but did not look away. 'Your friend said you were holding your abdomen…' A shudder passed through him. 'Mr Harrison,' Eleanor said gently, 'won't you let me just examine you?'

He stared at her for a long moment, and Eleanor thought he might attack her again; but all he said was, 'No.' Now it was her turn to hold his gaze. 'You'll hurt me,' he said, and there was real fear in his voice.

'Not if I can help it,' she coaxed. 'I can't help you unless I examine you.'

Again, silence. And then he nodded grudgingly. At Eleanor's urging, he heaved himself out of his chair and, blushing furiously, took off his breeches and stood before them in his underwear. Then he began to take off the belt he was using as a truss – the first, as it turned out, of many. They lay in a great pile of leather and brass at his feet. But he stopped before he was finished.

'And the last one,' prompted Eleanor.

'I can't take it off, Miss,' he said. 'Not unless I'm lying down. The pain's terrible.'

Eleanor glanced at Nurse Carr, who removed his jacket from the examination table. He lowered himself onto it and lay down. He hesitated, bracing himself, Eleanor supposed. His jaw clenched. He fumbled at the buckle, gasping all the while, then pulled it free and handed it to Nurse Carr. Without waiting to be asked, he yanked down his longjohns a little way, presumably to forestall Eleanor from doing so.

She stared at the distension of his abdomen, low down, near his groin. It was as bad as she had ever seen. 'Inguinal hernia,' she said to Nurse Carr, forcing herself to sound matter of fact. 'Some distension.' She turned to Frank. 'The pain comes from an obstruction in your bowel.' He looked close to panic. 'Probably caused by the hernia,' she said.

'But you're not going to touch me, are you, Miss?' He pulled up his longjohns again. 'You're just going to give me something for the pain,' he pleaded.

'We need to do something about the hernia straight away. It's already irreducible,' Eleanor said. Frank swung his legs over the edge of the table. 'Please don't stand up,' Eleanor said. He ignored her and got up. 'Let's just keep the weight off your abdomen until the operation.' That was a mistake.

Frank glared at her. 'There ain't going to be an operation.' He stumbled a few paces. 'You said you weren't going to touch me.' He looked around wildly. Sweat beaded his flushed skin and clung to his scrawny beard. 'Where's me trusses?' he demanded, but then thought better of it. 'Give me back me breeches,' he yelled.

He got them himself and put them on without bothering about the trusses, while Eleanor protested, 'You've already got an obstructed bowel. If the hernia strangulates…' He stopped what he was doing for a moment and stared at her blankly, clearly not understanding. 'You could be dead in hours,' Eleanor finished bluntly.

'You're a liar,' he snarled. 'A slip of a girl. What do you know?' He looked around. 'This hospital, it's a joke. And so are you, a joke.'

That hurt. 'Fetch Mr Bentley, please, Nurse Carr,' Eleanor said stiffly.

'Let you put the knife in me?' Frank said, ignoring her. He pulled the truss tight. The pain must have come over him then for he doubled over. 'Bastard,' he screamed. He clutched his abdomen. 'Oh God.' He stumbled forward and swept a scalpel up off the side. Eleanor backed away. Her mouth was dry with fear and her pulse hammered at her wrists and temples. 'Give me something,' he snarled, still holding himself with his free hand. He slashed wildly at her.

Eleanor darted back. 'Your guts are going to go gangrenous if we don't operate,' she said as calmly as she could, wondering where Daniel was.

'That's a posh word for butcher,' Frank sneered. 'Give me something, you cow!'

Daniel hobbled in behind Frank. 'Right,' he said. 'You – out! On your way.' Eleanor felt herself start to breathe again.

Frank whirled round and jabbed the knife at Daniel, who jerked away just in time.

'I'm in agony,' Frank gasped. He turned and stared pleadingly at Eleanor out of pain-filled eyes, but the knife never wavered from Daniel.

'Either you go now,' Daniel said, balancing on his stump and his good leg and brandishing his crutch, 'or I stick you in the guts with this,' he said.

'Mr Bentley,' Eleanor said severely.

Frank slammed the crutch aside, sending Daniel spinning into the wall. Before he could recover, Frank grabbed Nurse Carr and pulled her to him. He tried to shove the knife against her neck but she rammed her elbow into his stomach. He grunted and collapsed forward as Daniel yanked her away from Frank.

Frank fell against the table. 'Morphine,' he wept. 'Give us some morphine.'

No-one moved.

'No,' Eleanor said at last.

Frank stared at her for a moment longer. Then he grabbed the trusses off the table and backed away clutching them to his chest. The scalpel glinted. 'I'll get you,' he hissed. His jaw worked. 'I'll be back and I'll have that one.' He jabbed the knife at Eleanor.

'You do and I'll shove your trusses up your arse,' Daniel said.

I have to be the one in control, Eleanor thought. Not the patients, not Daniel. 'The knife, Mr Harrison,' she said, though it took all her courage.

He looked at it for a moment then threw it down. It clattered on the floor. He turned and limped away.

Eleanor leaned against the table. Scamps and rogues, her father had said. He had been right; and yet she had to prove him wrong – at least prove that she could cope.

'Nurse Carr,' she said after a moment, 'would you send in the next patient please?'

Chapter 7

Eleanor returned home a little after two o'clock. She had barely begun to unpin her hat when Kate rushed up. 'She's here, Miss,' she said. She was clutching a parasol with a fluffy pink ruffle round the top and an even pinker decorative handle. 'Look at this, Miss,' she said, holding it out. 'One of them French ones, she said.'

'Lovely,' Eleanor said, eyeing the thing cautiously. She followed Kate to Father's consulting room.

Miss Peggy Heart turned out to be almost exactly what Eleanor had expected: over forty, overperfumed and overdressed. And no matter what Father had said, she seemed no better than she should be. She was also, Eleanor judged, far too used to over-indulging in alcohol. Her ankles were puffy but her heart was strong and her blood pressure about right for her age. Dropsy, Eleanor thought with disgust. Nothing more than dropsy. She said as much to Miss Heart and advised her to rest and stop drinking, then showed her out.

'So,' Miss Heart said as they walked to the door, 'if I stop working and living, I'll be fit enough to go on working and living, is that it?'

'Moderation, Miss Heart. That's what I recommend,'

Eleanor said, refusing to be charmed. She smiled but refused to allow any warmth into it.

Miss Heart fumbled in her purse. 'Five shillings, I believe?' She pressed a coin into Eleanor's hands. 'I hope that this is the start of your fortune and that when you have rooms in Harley Street, I'll be able to say, "I gave her her first fee".'

Eleanor's smile grew chillier. She handed Miss Heart her parasol. The woman had completely misunderstood her aspirations.

'Thank you,' Miss Heart said. 'Your Dad said I'd be impressed with all your science and I certainly am. Thank you, Doctor. Goodbye.' She thrust out her hand.

Eleanor shook it. 'Goodbye, Miss Heart,' she said and opened the door.

She managed to refrain from scowling until she had closed it behind Miss Heart. She turned and flipped the crown piece from one hand to the other. Then she marched to her father's consulting room, passing Kate on the way. 'Is there a patient with my father, Kate?' she asked.

'No, Miss,' Kate said. Eleanor strode through the lobby of the consulting room, where a few elderly gentlemen were waiting. 'But he's just setting up...' Kate called, scurrying after her. Eleanor ignored her and charged into the consulting room without knocking. 'An inhalation!' Kate finished from behind her.

The door slammed behind Eleanor. Her father looked round sharply, and the bottle of oil he was pouring into an inhalation pot spilled all over his sleeve and the table.

'For goodness' sake, Eleanor,' he said. 'Look at this sleeve.'

He held it up for her inspection, then went over to the sink and started to sponge it.

'That woman is about as frail as a carthorse,' Eleanor said.

'If you could learn to knock first and then talk in a coherent manner,' he said plaintively.

'Father, she has no desire whatsoever to improve her health,' Eleanor said. 'I was wasting my time and hers.'

'She said she was unwell.' Father picked up a towel and dabbed off the excess water.

'I won't have you going out on the highways and byways, coaxing people to come and pay me the odd five shillings.' Eleanor sighed. She pressed the crown coin into Father's hand. 'You'd better have this back,' she said more gently. It was impossible to stay angry with him for long. She patted his hand, then went to the far door, so as not to disturb the patients again.

'What's she got?' her father asked.

'Nothing between her ears but champagne bubbles,' Eleanor said tartly. Then she thought better of it, turned back and said, 'That oil will stain.' She smiled to let him know she was joking.

***

A day or two later, Eleanor was in the Thrift waiting room. There were a few workmen bringing in furniture, while others laid gas-pipes and Daniel cleaned out the chimney, all watched over by Lady Peters. There were also a few patients. Eleanor was talking to one of them, a young mother, about her child's foot, which Eleanor suspected of being clubbed, when the door crashed open.

Frank Harrison reeled in. He stood in the middle of the room with his mouth open in a wordless scream of anguish. Eleanor's eyes widened in dismay.

'Help me,' he said at last. 'Help me. I'm dying, like she said.'

Daniel hobbled over to him at double speed. 'Yeah,' he said. 'Well, not fast enough.' He shoved at Frank, but without leverage he couldn't move him. 'Come on, on your way.'

Eleanor stood up. 'Mr Bentley, leave him,' she called.

'You're barred from this place,' Daniel said, as if he hadn't heard. He grabbed Frank's shoulder.

Lady Peters came across the room. 'Is this man drunk?' she demanded.

'He's in pain,' Eleanor said without looking at her. 'Mr Harrison,' she said, 'will you let me treat you?'

'Morphine,' he said. He stretched out a filthy hand to her. 'Give me the bloody morphine.'

Lady Peters tutted indignantly. 'I think we've heard quite enough,' she said. Eleanor did not dare take her gaze from Frank Harrison, but she could well imagine the look of indignation on Lady Peters' face. 'Mr Bentley?' the older woman said.

Daniel grabbed Frank's shoulder again, and this time he jerked him hard.

'And if we give you some, what about the operation?' Eleanor asked.

'Just give me the sodding stuff,' he snarled. Sweat, or perhaps tears, glinted on his cheeks. He yanked himself free from Daniel. 'And keep your hands off me!' It was clear his words were as much for Eleanor as Daniel.

Eleanor nodded to Daniel.

'Give us a hand,' he said to two of the men waiting to be seen.

Between them, they grabbed Frank and dragged him backwards out of the room, screaming as he went. Eleanor gazed after him. She swallowed hard.

'Come along,' Nurse Carr said to one of the patients. 'The doctor will be with you shortly.'

Whatever his faults, whatever he'd done, he'd been in so much pain...

'Are we paying you to stand and stare? I think not!' Lady Peters said to the workmen.

Surely no doctor could leave him like that?

'And when he cries, is he in pain with it or what?' Eleanor looked round at the woman who spoke and saw the mother with the clubfooted baby staring up at her from under her tatty straw hat. For a moment, she thought the girl was talking about Frank. 'Only,' the girl said, 'I can't bear to think of him in pain and helpless.'

'He's not in pain,' Eleanor said. 'Bring him back in three months.' Then she hurried out of the door after Frank.

Lady Peters was writing at the desk in the hallway. 'Eleanor?' she said as Eleanor rushed by.

'I can't leave him to die,' she said, already half-way out of the door.

'If he sobers up and is prepared to behave himself...' Lady Peters protested. Eleanor ignored her and went on outside.

She found Frank sprawled in the street a few hundred yards away, near a cluster of costermongers' barrows. The cobbles near his face were stained bright green with vomit. Eleanor gathered up her skirts and squatted down next to him. A clatter of wood on the cobbles made her look up. Daniel was hobbling as fast as he could down the street towards them. She smiled at him briefly, then turned her attention back to Frank.

'Do let us help you,' she begged. He stared at her blankly, all the fight gone out of him. 'You won't know anything about it,' she went on. 'We'll get an anaesthetist, someone to help you sleep all through the whole thing, I promise.'

'I'll die, won't I?' Frank was weeping openly now. The tears made tracks in the grime on his face. 'Whatever happens, I'm going to die.' He could barely get the words out.

'Not if you let me operate,' she insisted. 'The hernia's so swollen it can't slip back into your abdomen. All I have to do is make a single cut, slip it back in and sew you up again as good as new.' Frank whimpered. 'Look at me, Mr Harrison,' she said. He raised his head a bit, though it seemed to cause him a lot of pain. 'I tell you honestly,' she said, with all the sincerity she could bring to it, 'I haven't lost a single hernia patient yet.'

'No?' he muttered.

'Not one,' she said. It was the truth, after its own fashion. Frank winced and lowered his head to the stones. Eleanor took it for assent. 'Mr Bentley,' she said, 'get some of those men to bring out one of the bed frames. We'll get him back inside and lying down.'

Eleanor waited till they came, then hurried in ahead of them. She pulled on her jacket while she instructed Nurse Carr in how to prepare the consulting room for the operation. The men brought Frank Harrison in, who was still moaning. Lady Peters looked on disapprovingly.

'And give him some opium to calm him down,' Eleanor said as an afterthought. She got the bottle out of the locking cupboard and handed it to Nurse Carr. 'A full dose,' she said. 'I'll find an anaesthetist. Just keep him still.'

'What if no-one'll come?' Nurse Carr said. It was the first time Eleanor had heard her display any sign of nervousness.

'Someone will,' she said, wishing she felt as confident as she sounded. She hurried towards the door but Lady Peters stopped her.

'We're meeting the Bishop this afternoon,' she said. Eleanor stared at her in horror. She had quite forgotten. 'Four o'clock, Eleanor,' Lady Peters said, clearly exasperated. The tall feather on her black and lilac hat bounced, as if with indignation.

'I'll be there,' promised Eleanor.

'I hope so,' Lady Peters said. 'And mind what you say to him. He's not one of your raucous medical students.'

'I'll be a proper gentlewoman – not a word about blood and gore,' Eleanor said. Lady Peters looked shocked, as if she hadn't even considered that as a possibility. 'I promise,' Eleanor soothed her. In the consulting room, Frank Harrison yelped with pain. Eleanor looked back at him anxiously. 'Now, excuse me – I really must go.'

It was not far to the East London Hospital from the Thrift. Eleanor walked as fast as she could, but this time it seemed to take hours to get there.

She found her objective – Doctor Marsham – in the forecourt of the hospital, which was fortunate since she had not relished the idea of sneaking around its corridors.

'Mr Marsham,' she called when she caught sight of his gawky figure, dark as a crow against the pale granite of the hospital.

He turned and she dashed over to him. 'What do you want, Miss Bramwell?' he asked. He did not seem in the least pleased to see her.

'I have a man with a strangulated hernia,' she said. She was quite out of breath. 'He's dying. He needs surgery.'

Doctor Marsham started to walk away. 'Then you'd better find yourself a surgeon,' he snapped and strode away.

Eleanor hurried to keep up. 'I have,' she said. 'I just need an anaesthetist.' He didn't slow or look at her. 'Please,' she begged, 'he'll die for the want of a few drops of ether.'

Doctor Marsham let out a great sigh. 'What surgeon have you got?' He turned abruptly and looked at her. When she didn't answer, he said, 'Oh no' and walked on.

'I've seen enough herniotomies,' Eleanor said, wishing it sounded less defensive.

Doctor Marsham turned again. 'For God's sake, woman!' he bellowed. Eleanor's eyes widened in shock. 'Can't his employers pay for him to come here?' he asked more quietly.

'He hasn't got a job,' Eleanor admitted. That was too much for Doctor Marsham. He stalked off, disgust plain on his face. Eleanor paced him. 'Are you going to let him die because you can't spare an hour and daren't risk your job?' He slowed. Eleanor stopped. 'He's the father of five little babies,' she called after him. He hesitated. 'Their only support.' Doctor Marsham still didn't turn. 'And such a nice, gentle man,' she added, not caring about the lie.

Doctor Marsham turned. His expression was a curious combination of irritation and resignation. 'You see what happens when you head off on your own? You get put into all sorts of impossible situations by all sorts of damned people.' He strode towards her. 'You brought this on yourself, you know that,' he demanded as he passed her.

Again, she was forced to hurry along beside him. 'Where are you going?' she asked.

'I don't know!' he shouted. 'I've never been to your damned Thrift. You'll have to lead the way.' He turned round and started back the way he'd been going in the first place.

Eleanor grabbed his arm and pulled him round, and together they ignored the stares of the ladies and gentlemen they passed as they ran back to the Thrift.

***

'It'll be like stuffing a struggling cat into a warm meat pie,' Doctor Marsham said once he had seen the patient.

'How vivid,' Eleanor said. She was at the sink in the small area off the consulting room, scrubbing her hands. She turned. At the other end of the room, Frank Harrison lay moaning on the scrubbed table, while Nurse Carr dabbed gingerly at his abdomen with a piece of lysol-soaked lint, which she held in a pair of forceps.

'Right,' said Doctor Marsham. 'What ether masks do you have?' Eleanor picked up a towel and waved it at him. He sighed. 'No mask?'

'We have plenty of ether.'

'Very well,' he said. 'We'll have to manage as best we can.'

Eleanor smiled, so grateful that he was there that she would have forgiven him any amount of grumpiness.

She went through into the treatment room. Doctor Marsham followed her, carrying the towel. Frank Harrison lay on the table, grizzling softly to himself, while Daniel watched him with undisguised dislike and Nurse Carr spread rags on the floor to soak up the blood. Eleanor went to check the instruments. Scalpels, she thought – there should be three.

Retractors. Her hands were shaking. I'm not nervous, she thought. I'm not. Scissors. Lint, needles, catgut. If she weren't nervous, why was her stomach fluttering?

'Ready?' Doctor Marsham asked from behind her.

She spun round. He had a piece of lint in his hand and was holding the bottle ready to soak it with ether. She swallowed hard. 'Yes,' she said.

Doctor Marsham dribbled ether onto the lint.

'What's this then?' Frank muttered. 'Wha's that?'

Doctor Marsham pressed the rolled-up towel over Frank's face but the big man began to struggle. His whimpers turned to high-pitched little screams and he flailed around. Daniel leaned over him and tried to hold him down but was thrown off.

'I'm going to die, I'm going to die,' wailed Frank.

Doctor Marsham reached for more ether, then thought better of it. 'Damn it,' he exclaimed. 'Ether's too slow for this one. Chloroform, quick!' Nurse Carr hurried to get it. 'Have you got any chloroform?' he bellowed as Frank kept up his screaming. Nurse Carr came back with the bottle and poured it directly onto the towel he held out. Doctor Marsham leaned across Frank and pressed the towel to his face while Daniel did his best to hold down his arms. Within seconds, Frank had quietened down.

Daniel stood up to let Eleanor have some room. She picked up the largest scalpel and surveyed the vast, hairy expanse of Frank's abdomen. Now, she thought; but she didn't move. The scalpel felt as heavy as lead in her hand.

'I don't know how long we'll keep him under,' Doctor Marsham said.

Now, Eleanor thought again. This time, she forced herself

to move forward and stretch Frank's flesh between her fingers. The scalpel shook in her hand.

'Be ready with the sponges, Nurse,' she said.

'Of course, Doctor,' Nurse Carr said.

Eleanor pressed the blade to Frank's skin. It gave under the pressure but the scalpel didn't cut it. She took a deep breath and pressed harder. A bead of blood appeared. She moved the scalpel and the bead became a line. I can do this, she thought triumphantly. I can do this.

***

Ten minutes later, she wasn't so sure. She had made the incision correctly. All that remained to be done was to push Frank Harrison's intestines back into his abdomen; but they wouldn't go.

'Go in,' she growled at them. She was bloodied up to her elbows and her hair was coming free of its pins and was lank with sweat. 'Go in... Can't you make me some more room with those retractors?' she snapped at Nurse Carr.

'If you'd make a bigger incision, Doctor,' Nurse Carr snapped back, though Eleanor had made it plain that she wanted to limit the possibility of infection.

'Here,' Doctor Marsham said. 'I'll take this one.' He eased one of the retractors out of Nurse Carr's grasp. 'You pull on that one as hard as you can.' Nurse Carr pulled a bit harder. 'He can take it,' Doctor Marsham urged.

'That's better,' Eleanor said. 'Come on, you slippery, slippery...' The intestines writhed obscenely, like crimson and purple snakes.

'Shove it in, Doctor,' Doctor Marsham said tetchily. 'Shove it in.'

'There has to be some degree of care,' Eleanor snarled.

Then, suddenly, she had it. They slid back into place and she was done. She looked up triumphantly, only to see Daniel staring at her. He looked so nauseous that she feared he might be their next patient. She smiled at him and wiped her hands. It took only a few minutes to suture the wound, and then they were able – with some difficulty – to move Frank back to a bed in the ward.

While Nurse Carr made him comfortable, Eleanor and Doctor Marsham cleaned themselves up.

'Nurse Carr is sitting with him tonight,' Eleanor said, scrubbing at her arms. 'She'll sleep when she can. I'll have to bring someone in tomorrow.'

'Well, he's made it thus far, thanks to your determination,' Doctor Marsham said.

Eleanor smiled at the compliment. 'I didn't realize how exhausting it would be,' she said, pushing a strand of errant hair out of her eyes with the back of her hand. 'Perhaps next time I'll hold the towel and you can do the hard work,' she teased.

His face lit up with an uncharacteristic excitement, and she knew she had made a mistake. 'If that's a serious offer…' he said.

'I'm sorry, it isn't,' Eleanor said. 'But we do need you as an anaesthetist.' She dried her hands on the towel hanging by the basin.

A look of disappointment flashed across his face and was gone. 'Ah well,' he said heavily. 'I'm already an anaesthetist.' He tried a smile. 'Like you, I want to be a surgeon.'

'There won't be enough operations to occupy both of us.'

Eleanor felt she at least owed him an explanation. 'I'm only going to have six beds.'

'I know.' He sounded resigned, though not as if he held it against her, and Eleanor reminded herself that he had almost as hard a struggle at the East London as she had had. 'Can I come back and see if he recovers?' he asked as he picked up his coat.

'Of course,' Eleanor said. 'I'll walk along with you. I have to meet a Bishop about some money.' She took off her apron and threw it into the laundry basket, then rolled down her sleeves. 'And I am – I really am – very grateful.'

Doctor Marsham smiled his habitual, sour smile. 'That makes me feel much better,' he said, pulling on his jacket. His tone was light but there was a barb in it he couldn't quite disguise. 'When I'm sixty and still pouring ether over some labourer's face, and still living in rooms, I'll remember your gratitude with gratitude.' He walked off, leaving Eleanor wondering quite what she should make of it.

Chapter 8

Eleanor rushed into Lady Peters' drawing room without even stopping to take off her coat. She hadn't thought to look at her watch until she was almost there, and she had been shocked to discover that it was a quarter to five. She turned and pushed her medical bag into the maid's hands, though she held on to the paper-wrapped bottle she was carrying in her other hand.

'Lady Peters,' she said. 'Your Grace.'

The Bishop stood up. He was a thin, little man, white-haired and clean shaven but with fuzzy mutton-chops down to his jaw.

Eleanor hurried over and plumped herself down at the tea table. She surveyed the remains of tea with dismay.

'Your Grace,' Lady Peters said. 'This, at last, is Doctor Eleanor Bramwell.'

Eleanor and the Bishop shook hands. 'Delighted, Miss Bramwell.' He peered at her curiously, as if she were some exotic species of butterfly.

Once he sat back down, Eleanor said, 'We had our first operation to perform.' That reminded her of the bottle she was carrying. She twisted round in her seat and put it carefully on the windowsill behind her. 'And it was rather…' she hesitated, suddenly mindful of her promise to be the perfect gentlewoman. 'It took longer than we expected.'

'Then you should have left it till this evening,' Lady Peters said sharply.

'With some poor soul in such need, it must be difficult to turn your back,' the Bishop said.

Eleanor smiled at him gratefully. 'Specially when you've got the patient opened up before you realize that the Bishop is already waiting.' She smiled at him, and saw that he was almost – not quite, but almost – smiling back. Lady Peters, on the other hand, was glaring at her. She poured tea for herself. 'I am sorry,' she went on. 'I do hope that you'll come and visit us soon, see how much our little infirmary needs your Sunday fund.'

'Do you promise not to frighten a poor cleric if I do?' the Bishop asked gravely. For a moment Eleanor was fooled. Then she saw the gleam in his eye and realized, with some relief, that he was teasing.

***

Eleanor knocked on the door of her father's consulting room and entered without waiting for an answer. He was heating a test-tube over a Bunsen burner.

'Do you have the specific gravity meter?' She flourished the bottle she'd had at Lady Peter's. Father nodded in the direction of the cupboard but kept moving the test-tube over the flame. 'Good,' Eleanor said, going to get it. 'My hernia man isn't the healthiest.'

'You've carried that all the way from the Thrift?' Father asked, somewhat shocked.

'Took it to Lady Peters' drawing room, too,' Eleanor said, relishing his reaction. She took the equipment over to the table to work.

He stared gloomily at the test-tube. 'My daughter, the well-known eccentric,' he said.

'I get it from you, if I am,' Eleanor pointed out. She set the box on the table and began to get the equipment ready. 'Look at us – a lovely evening and here we are, testing urine together.'

Father poured a reagent into the test-tube. 'Well, it's not the best social life, I admit.'

'I've been neglecting you, haven't I?' Eleanor asked gently. 'All caught up with the Thrift.' She poured Frank Harrison's urine into the flask from the specific gravity meter. 'How long is it since you went to the music hall?' She stoppered the urine bottle and answered her own question. 'Weeks and weeks.'

'I've been very busy,' Father said. He seemed slightly embarrassed, Eleanor thought. Well, she supposed it must seem a bit off, a grown man having to depend on his daughter for his socializing. 'I've got a lot of work to do.'

'Nonsense,' said Eleanor. She took the brass specific gravity meter out of its velvet-lined box. 'I'm taking you to the theatre tomorrow evening.' She eased the meter into the flask of urine. 'I don't suppose my mother would have left you languishing here night after night, and neither will I.'

Father smiled and didn't argue any more, so that was settled.

***

There was, it seemed, at least one person who loved Frank Harrison. She arrived mid-morning, a stout scarecrow of a woman, with a frizz of red hair around a face raw with broken veins. She hurried over to Frank, who was propped up in bed, and clasped his hand to her ample bosom.

Eleanor remembered what Frank's friend had said when he

had first brought the man in, and realized that this must be Polly. She didn't look so very terrifying, considering that the mere mention of her name had made Frank pause in the middle of his alcohol-driven rage.

Terrifying or not, she was still there when Doctor Marsham arrived to see how the patient was doing. He seemed pleased enough that Frank was doing so well, but he stood at the end of the bed and said sternly, 'A man with your responsibilities can't afford to leave this world early.' Frank stared at him blankly and Polly didn't seem to follow any better either. It was hardly surprising considering the little exaggeration Eleanor had indulged in. Still, there was no stopping Doctor Marsham, so she supposed she'd just have to make the best of it. 'But, thanks to Doctor Bramwell, you have every chance of looking after your children for many years to come.'

'Fat chance,' Frank said to Eleanor's dismay. 'Let them look after theirselves.'

Polly beamed up at them as if her man had made the most eloquent speech of thanks. 'Bless them,' she said, slurring her words just a little, 'wherever they are.'

Eleanor bit her lip, then forced herself to stop, thankful that Doctor Marsham didn't seem to have noticed.

'Your five little children,' he probed.

'Two, Sir. Grown up, now,' Frank said. At least now that he was sober and pain-free, he was genial.

Doctor Marsham glanced sharply at Eleanor, but by then she'd managed to compose herself. 'You won't be able to do any heavy manual work in the future,' she said to change the subject.

'Suits me, Miss,' Frank said cheerfully. 'I hate the bleeding stuff.' He cackled.

Polly smiled at her, revealing a mouthful of caries. 'He's not made for it,' she said. 'Well, you can see that for yourself.' She patted him affectionately on the shoulder.

'I want to say I'm sorry,' Frank said quietly. Don't say it, Eleanor thought at him. Just don't say… 'For the fighting and that.' Eleanor managed to keep her smile fixed in place, but it took an effort of will. Surely it couldn't get any worse? It did. 'When I've been on the bevvy, you know,' he finished.

'He's only human,' Polly said. She twisted round and her bag clinked suggestively.

At least they had the grace to look embarrassed. Perhaps that was why Frank went on, 'I got carried away, but I shouldn't have gone for you, Miss.'

That, finally, was too much for Doctor Marsham. 'You attacked Doctor Bramwell?' he asked levelly.

'It was a scuffle,' Eleanor put in. 'Really, it was nothing.'

If looks could have killed, Doctor Marsham would have been guilty of the murder of Frank Harrison on the spot.

'I'm a drunken rogue, Miss,' Frank said. 'But I would never harm you.' He smiled at her sweetly, and she realized he meant it. 'You remind me of me first wife, Miss,' he said. He chuckled. 'Till her teeth fell out.' He guffawed and so did Polly. Eleanor found she was grinning.

Doctor Marsham ended the moment. 'Doctor Bramwell has scruples about allowing someone like you to die,' he said. Eleanor glanced at him, wishing she could say something to stop him, but he was obviously furious. 'I have no such scruples, and if you so much as raise your voice I will personally throw you out onto the street, wound and all.' He glared at the pair of them till the smiles died on their faces. 'Do you understand me?'

Frank licked his lips. 'Yes, Sir,' he said. 'Sorry, Sir.' Polly wouldn't look at them at all.

'You are here as a charity case and you will behave like one,' Doctor Marsham said. He stormed off.

Eleanor hurried after him. It seemed to be the only thing she ever did. 'I had to say something to get you here,' she said desperately. If he wouldn't be their anaesthetist, she was going to have a terrible time finding someone else. Besides, she liked him, dour Scots moods and all. 'And he's a harmless old thing really.'

'You're an innocent, Miss Bramwell,' he said. 'But it won't last long in this place.'

He sounded just like her father, only without the sense of humour, she thought. She wondered if it would be better to let him calm down before she tried to talk to him – that usually worked best with Father. But if he went she'd have to brave the East London again, and even if she did he might refuse to see her.

She touched him on the arm. 'I've been thinking about you still being an anaesthetist when you're sixty,' she said. He turned round and glared at her. She hurried on, 'When we get the Bishop's Sunday fund, will you come as an anaesthetist for two mornings a week, for a fee?'

'I've already told you – no,' he said, drowning out her last few words.

'And as a surgeon, for no fee, on one,' she finished despite him. 'You'll have to take whatever cases I've got waiting, but…'

94

'Surgery?' he said. His smile lit up his face. 'One morning a week?'

Eleanor smiled back. Not a bad start to the day after all, she thought.

***

That night, she took Father to the music hall. It was a pleasant enough way to spend the night, she supposed, if you ignored the heat and the smell of bodies, gin and cigars, and the rough housing up in the gods, but she could take it or leave it.

Conjurers, tumblers, comedians and singers came and went. Then at last it was time for the star turn, Miss Peggy Heart. *The* Miss Peggy Heart, Father had called her, as if everyone knew her name; and indeed the audience clapped and cheered and huzzahed as she came on stage. She was wearing a low-cut red dress and a many-stranded diamond – or more likely diamante – choker that drew the eye to her ample bosoms. She twirled a flounced parasol that would have driven Kate into ecstacies of delight.

She sang a song and then another, with the audience joining in at every opportunity. She had a good, if somewhat gin, husky voice and she knew how to put herself around the stage.

So this is what she does that prevents her attending to her health, Eleanor thought. She could not quite bring herself to join in, though Father was, without the least trace of embarrassment.

'Hello,' she sang, at the start of 'Who's Your Lady Friend?'

'Hello,' chorused the audience. Eleanor glanced at Father. He was enjoying himself more than he had for a long time. She decided she should be less of an old sourpuss and join in too. She'd probably draw less attention to herself that way, in any case.

'It isn't the girl I saw you with at Brighton,' Peggy Heart sang. She whirled round, holding the parasol high. 'Who?' She looked expectantly at the audience.

'Who?' they carolled back, Eleanor among them.

'Who?' sang Miss Heart.

'Who?' Eleanor realized she was enjoying herself. And Miss Heart was good at what she did, for what it was worth.

'Who's your lady friend?' She shut the parasol and the audience clapped and cheered.

She came forward and dipped a curtsy. 'What shall we end the evening with?' she asked.

There was an uproar of suggestions, not all of them things decent people might suggest. Peggy Heart waited a moment, then cupped a hand to her ear.

'"A Little of What You Fancy",' someone shouted.

'"The Boy I Love is Up in the Gallery",' called someone else.

'I can't hear you,' shouted Miss Heart.

'"Ta-Ra-Ra-Boom-De-Ay",' Father shouted. To her surprise, Eleanor saw that Peggy Heart was looking straight at him.

'"Ta-Ra-Ra-Boom-De-Ay" it will be, Sir,' Peggy Heart said, with a little dip of her skirt. She tossed her head archly, whirled round and held up her parasol. It was a popular choice and gained a lot of applause.

Father settled back in his seat. Eleanor glanced at him. He was smiling so...tenderly. There was no other word for it. And the way he'd looked at Miss Heart...she'd seemed almost to be waiting for him to choose.

No, she thought. It was ridiculous.

'A smart and stylish girl you see,' Peggy Heart chanted without accompaniment, 'the belle of good society. Not too strict but rather free, yet as right as right can be.' She closed her parasol and brought it round in front of her, bending low over it in one smooth movement, revealing rather more of her cleavage than was seemly. 'Not too young and not too old, not too timid, not too bold…' She turned and came to the front of the stage. 'Just the kind you'd like to hold,' she rubbed her arm in a way that left little to the imagination. There was a roar of approval from the rough housers in the gallery. 'Just the kind for sport, I'm told…' The rough housers weren't the only ones cheering, Eleanor noted drily. At least Father was only watching.

There was a pause, and then the orchestra struck up the tune. 'Ta-Ra-Ra-Boom-De-Ay,' Miss Heart sang, and whirled round. 'Ta-Ra-Ra-Boom-De-Ay, Ta-Ra-Ra-Boom-De-Ay,' she whirled and whirled, and the audience sang along. Eleanor glanced at her father, only to find that he was looking at her. She smiled, to show she was enjoying herself. 'Ta-Ra-Ra-Boom-.' Miss Heart whirled round again. She held her hands up and opened her mouth but no sound came out.

Eleanor's father stood up. They are after all, friends, Eleanor told herself firmly. She started to push her way to the end of the row. Her father followed.

Miss Heart's face was flushed. She clutched at her stomach, then coughed. Blood spurted out of her mouth and covered her creamy skin. She reeled forward. One step. Another. Then she sank to the stage, with the blood still pouring out of her mouth.

The audience was in chaos as people tried to get a better

look or wanted to know what was happening. Eleanor reached the stage. Miss Heart was slumped over; her chin and chest and hands were covered in blood. She stared at Eleanor with huge, fearful eyes.

'Bring the curtain down,' the Master of Ceremonies shouted.

'Send for some ice,' Eleanor instructed him. She hurried over to the stricken woman. 'Lower the curtain,' she said over her shoulder as she helped Miss Heart lie down. 'Lie still,' she said to Miss Heart. 'Try not to cough.'

None of the theatre staff had moved. Eleanor looked up to see her father staring at her – or, perhaps, at Peggy Heart.

'Get some ice,' he commanded the MC. 'And bring that curtain down now.' The curtain finally fell. In the half-dark, Eleanor crouched down and listened to her patient's heart while her father looked on.

Chapter 9

The carriage ride from Argyle Street to Islington seemed to take forever, especially since they dared not go above a fast walking pace for fear of jolting Miss Heart.

Eleanor ran up the steps and hammered at the door. She explained to Kate what had happened and told her to get the butler to help bring Miss Heart into the house.

Kate held open the door.

'The guest room, Kate?' Eleanor asked as she went in. 'Is it ready?'

'Yes of course, Miss,' Kate said, standing back to let the men in with Miss Heart. 'There's no fire,' she added.

'Careful of her head,' Father said as they took Miss Heart upstairs. The ice pack she was clutching to her throat was melting and the cold water had smeared her make-up. Her colour was not good. She stared around her wide-eyed, clearly shocked if not actually in shock.

Eleanor watched them go up, then turned back. 'Kate, dressings – old sheets, anything you can find.' The groom had followed them in. He did not usually come into the upper part of the house and stood timidly holding out Father's top hat and cane. Eleanor took them. 'I need ice, lots and lots of ice.' He ambled off. 'Go to Billingsgate,' Eleanor shouted. 'Run!'

She hurried up to the guest room, passing the butler on his way back down. Inside, Father was tucking a pillow behind Miss Heart's head.

Eleanor rushed to help him and together they began to get Miss Heart's cape off. She gasped and whimpered.

'It's not a pulmonary haemorrhage,' Father said as he worked.

'No, I don't think so,' agreed Eleanor. 'Her lungs seem clear.' She finally pulled the cape free. 'The ice helps.'

Father moved away. Eleanor helped Miss Heart sit up and started to unlace her dress at the back. Kate moved in and began to clean the blood off her face.

Miss Heart pulled her arm out of the sleeve of her dress. As she did so, she spotted Father. 'Send him out,' she said.

'Miss Heart,' Eleanor said, 'we must get you into bed, have you lying down.'

'Out!'

'Peggy,' Father said. Eleanor's eyes widened in shock. 'My dear…' There was such tenderness in his voice that she turned to look at him. She swallowed hard. She didn't have to think about it now. There was work to be done.

Miss Heart clutched her cape to her bosom. 'Don't let him see me like this,' she pleaded. She was weeping. 'A lady needs a bit of dignity.'

'Father, please?' Eleanor said, poker-faced. He nodded. 'Could you get the 'scope?' Eleanor asked as he got to the door.

He had looked so worried…so much more worried than one would for any ordinary patient. Again, Eleanor pushed it to the back of her mind. She unclipped Miss Heart's dress, wondering if the woman could possibly have cinched herself any tighter with a block and tackle.

'I don't want him to see me like this,' Miss Heart said.

'He is a doctor,' Eleanor pointed out.

'Never let a man see you at your worst,' Miss Heart answered, through sobs that were becoming almost hysterical. She clutched Eleanor's hand and held it tight.

Perhaps that's all it is, Eleanor thought. If your whole life depended on how you looked, perhaps there came to be no difference between one man and another.

Yes, she thought. That would be it. 'Don't try to talk,' she said, helping Miss Heart lie down. 'Just lie still.'

Eleanor gave her some ice to suck and sat holding her hand until she quietened down.

A little while later there was a quiet tap at the door. Eleanor extricated her hand from Miss Heart's and slipped outside, closing the door softly behind her.

Her father stood on the landing. 'Is there anything you need?'

'No,' Eleanor whispered, not moving from the doorway. 'She's quite calm now.'

'You won't forget to keep renewing the ice?'

'Of course, Father.' He looked tired and worried. 'I do know what to do,' she chided gently. He might know she was qualified, but to him she would always be his daughter and in need of support.

'Well, I'll be in my study if you need me.' He started down the stairs.

'There's no need to stay up,' Eleanor said. There was nothing that could be done for Miss Heart that two doctors could do better than one. Perhaps he thought she would want a second opinion.

He bit his lip. 'I prefer to,' he said. 'Just in case…' There it was again.

He got to the top of the stairs before she had to ask. 'How well do you know Miss Heart?'

'Hardly at all,' he said. He looked at her levelly. 'I admire her voice.' He paused, as if searching for the right words. 'Her…vitality.'

Eleanor watched him go downstairs. He was her father. If he said he hardly knew the woman, that had to be the truth. Had to be.

***

Next morning, Miss Heart was calm enough to allow Eleanor to examine her. She was as different as could be from the woman who had strutted the stage of the Argyle Theatre. Her gorgeous red hair – nothing more than an expensive wig – lay piled up on the dresser. Her own was more grey than black, and hung over her shoulder in a thin plait. Her skin, bereft of powder and paint, was pallid and had a yellowish tinge, except that her cheeks were blotched red with broken veins. The delicate areas round her mouth and eyes were etched with fine lines. Eleanor increased her estimate of Miss Heart's age by ten years, at least.

Eleanor listened to her heart and percussed it; then she examined her abdomen. When Miss Heart had rearranged her nightdress and got back under the blankets, Eleanor examined her throat. She peered down it. There was plenty of early-morning sun that day, and with the help of a mirror on a rod and the laryngoscope – a circular mirror tied round her forehead – she was able to get a good enough view to confirm the opinion she had already formed. To be certain, when she was done she checked the inners of Miss Heart's lower eyelids.

'Thank you,' she said when she was done. She unfastened the laryngoscope and packed it away in its rosewood box.

'What do you think?' Miss Heart asked.

'I think you should suck some more ice,' Eleanor said. The cold would stop the bleeding by narrowing the blood vessels, and also help to reduce any congestion, though in truth Eleanor no longer thought Miss Heart's lungs were the problem.

Miss Heart scooped up some ice from the dish on the bedside table. 'It all tastes of fish,' she complained but popped it into her mouth obediently. 'What's the sentence?'

'For now, I just want you to rest,' Eleanor said. There was no point worrying the woman until she was absolutely certain. She finished packing her things and stood up. 'I'll be back shortly.'

She felt Miss Heart watching her as she left the room. She knows I'm not telling her everything, she thought; but there was nothing to be done about it. She hurried downstairs to her father's consulting room and asked permission to look in his reference library.

'Well?' he said, after a time.

Eleanor looked up from the book she had found. He was sitting at the desk, by the window. The harsh morning light slanting in between the slats of the Venetian blinds silvered his hair and deepened the shadows beneath his eyes. He looked old – old and tired. Eleanor wondered whether he had had any sleep at all.

'It's unmistakeable,' she said. She took the book over to him to show him the reference she had found. 'The bleeding comes not from her throat but from her stomach.' She scowled.

103

'How I missed it...'

Her father stood up. 'Well, I've only ever seen it this bad once before myself,' he said. Eleanor nodded, a little reassured; she had thought he might blame her for missing something. 'Lord Colombo,' Father said. 'It was the drink with him.'

'I think it's the drink with her,' Eleanor said. Father looked shocked. 'Her liver feels enlarged,' she explained, as she went to put the book back in its place. 'She admits to drinking heavily, and under that make-up she's jaundiced.' She shut the glass doors of the bookcase and turned round. 'So, what did you do for Lord Colombo?'

Her father hesitated. 'Read an address at his funeral,' he said. In other circumstances it might almost have been a joke; but he was as solemn as the grave. Then he seemed to shake it off. 'Oh, it can't be the same for Miss Heart.' He started towards the door. 'I think I'd better examine her myself.'

Eleanor stopped him. 'She doesn't want you to see her, Father,' she said. He started to protest. 'She doesn't want you to see her,' Eleanor repeated. 'There really is no doubt at all.'

Her father scowled. 'Colombo was a fat, red-faced old sot,' he said; but he paced slowly back towards the window. He leaned on the desk. 'She's so...' he paused, as if searching for the right word, 'enchanting,' he said at last, without looking at Eleanor.

Enchanting? It was hardly the word she would have chosen. She fought to keep her composure, and won. 'She'll make a good recovery if only she'll do as she's advised.' She stopped. Swallowed. It was no good. She could no longer ignore what she'd seen and heard; what he had just said. 'Father, I hope that you and Miss Heart...' she stopped. She could not bring herself to say it, and now he was looking at her like a man expecting to hear a death sentence. Perhaps it was not Miss Heart. Perhaps it was someone else, someone more suitable, and somehow the events of the night had made him realize he must tell her. She began again, hoping she had found the right words. 'I hope you have not brought someone to my Mother's house who...'

'My house, Eleanor,' he put in sharply, standing up to face her.

She would not allow herself to be deflected. Must not. 'Someone', she drove on, 'who has some call on your affections.'

He had. She saw guilt written all over his face. 'I did not bring her here,' he said. 'I wouldn't have done so, but you took charge.'

'Her?' Eleanor whispered. 'Oh Father...' She spat out the words as if they were wormwood.

'Eleanor, I need no lectures.' He looked at her tiredly, then turned and picked up his coat. 'If you'll excuse me, I have a patient arriving at ten o'clock.'

He strode past her. She whirled round and demanded of his departing back, 'So a patient of mine, sleeping under this roof, is your...' She could not say the word, for fear it might choke her. 'Your what, Father? Mistress?'

He turned to face her. 'Thanks to your management of the situation she's here and we must take care of her,' he said. There was some truth in that, Eleanor supposed. He had seemed almost in a daze at the theatre and she had not hesitated to take command; she had thought to get Miss Heart somewhere quiet, somewhere where, if the worst happened, the equipment was available to look after her. Home had seemed the logical place. Her father took a deep breath. 'She came to you for help barely a week ago, but you were so busy disapproving of her that she got none.' His voice got louder and angrier with every word. He walked off. Eleanor stared after him, biting back tears. He turned. 'So don't you lecture me, young lady!' he shouted.

He's right, she thought after he had gone. He's right, but how could he do that to Mother's memory? To me?

***

Later, when she had recovered her composure, she went to see Miss Heart again. She might not like her. She might not approve of her. But she would not allow that, or anything, to cause her to behave unprofessionally.

'You must have no more drink,' she said. 'I do mean no more.' Her hands were folded neatly in her lap and she managed to keep her voice cool and calm. 'And you need rest. You have to stop singing.'

'I can't give up singing,' Miss Heart protested. She sounded truly shocked.

'You must be able to do other work,' Eleanor said, unperturbed.

'I've worked the halls since I was eight,' Miss Heart said. Eleanor supposed it had been that or chimney sweeping, or a life on the streets, or somesuch. 'You don't know what my audience means to me.' She smiled.

'You could have died last night,' Eleanor said, letting her voice grow even colder. If the woman thought she could be charmed as her father had been, she was mistaken. 'The audience was in uproar. If they mean anything at all to you, you won't want to risk a repeat performance.' It was cruel, but

Miss Heart was either too stupid or too insensitive to understand anything but the crudest stimuli; and if she were to be saved she had to come to realize what she must do.

But the response she provoked was one she neither expected nor desired. 'You don't think very much of me, do you?' Eleanor flushed. She had not thought she was so transparent or that Miss Heart was capable of such insight. 'You think I'm loud and vulgar and foolish.' She leaned forward. 'But I make an honest living being loud and vulgar. It's what the men want.'

Eleanor stiffened. 'Some, it appears.' Her tone was arctic.

Now it was Miss Heart's turn to be shocked. So, Eleanor thought, it's all in the open now; I know, and she knows I know.

'Most of them,' Miss Heart said gently. 'All sorts of men.' If it were intended to hurt, it succeeded.

'I care only for your health, not your morals,' snapped Eleanor. She regretted it immediately, not because it had, perhaps, been less than kind, but because it revealed that she had been hurt. She stood up. 'I'll send Kate in with your tea.' She swept out without another word.

Downstairs, she dressed for the street. Her father came out of his room while she was fastening her cape.

'Are you going to the Thrift?' he asked. Eleanor nodded. It would be a relief to be out of the house; she would simply not think about the two of them left alone together. 'Is she safe to leave?' Father asked quietly.

If the anger had gone out of him, it had not left her. 'I do have other patients,' she snapped.

'You still think it's alcohol with her?' It wasn't really a question.

107

'She has all the stigmata of liver disease,' Eleanor said. She could not look at him. 'She's a drinker', she added bluntly and then, before she could stop herself, 'among other things.' The thought of those other things sickened her.

'She's vivacious, defiant, brave and warm,' Father said quietly. 'Most of all, she's warm.'

Eleanor felt her face flush. She turned on him. 'You've always said my mother was warm,' she said. Her voice shook. How dare he compare that…that bawd with her mother. His wife.

He sat down slowly on the chair by the hall table. 'So she was. She was,' he murmured. He looked up at her, and his eyes were ineffably weary, ineffably sad. 'Time will come when being a doctor isn't enough even for you.' Eleanor opened her mouth to protest, but he went on, 'You could learn a great deal from Peggy Heart, if ever you got down from your high horse long enough.'

I will not cry, Eleanor thought. I will not cry in front of him. She realized she was shaking. 'I have promised Miss Heart that you will respect her privacy,' she said, far more coldly than she had intended. 'In the circumstances it would seem wise.'

'Go and see your Bishop, Eleanor,' Father said. 'You have much in common.'

***

By the time Eleanor got to the Thrift she had managed to compose herself. Lady Peters was already there, dressed today in plain black though the feather in her hat was jaunty. Doctor Marsham was there too – after all, the Bishop's Sunday fund might well pay his wage.

The Bishop arrived a little after Eleanor, resplendent in his long, purple, ecclesiastical robes. Nurse Carr and Doctor Marsham waited a little way off while Eleanor and Lady Peters talked to the Bishop. They led him into the waiting room, where a few patients were reading their Bibles in silence. It was one of Lady Peters' more inspired touches. Another was the sign she had hung up, listing the Thrift's regulations, including prayers twice a day.

'Hopefully,' the Bishop said, looking around him, 'when you have your wards open, there'll be some moral guidance for your patients? For if we tend only the body and neglect the soul…'

'As we're in your diocese, we would hope for some religious guidance from you and your ministers,' Lady Peters said.

The Bishop smiled. 'I can see that this infirmary will soon be a jewel in the crown of Christianity.'

Eleanor smiled, hoping it was not unworthy of her to hope that it would soon be a better funded jewel. 'Although our ward is not yet open, we do have one surgical patient.' She beckoned to Doctor Marsham. He came over. 'Doctor Marsham acted as my anaesthetist in a life-saving operation.'

'Doctor,' the Bishop acknowledged. He put out a hand like a bird's claw.

Doctor Marsham shook it. 'Your Grace,' he said, bowing.

'The ward is this way,' Eleanor said, leading the way. 'You'll see that the patient is, post-operatively, still very weak and drowsy,' she said as they walked through the kitchen, 'but essentially well.'

She smiled at the Bishop, then turned…to see Frank's bed empty and in disarray, while Polly lay sprawled in a drunken stupor on the one next to it.

'Oh ain't it a pity she's only one titty to suckle the baby on?' Frank's voice bellowed – Eleanor could not bring herself to call it singing – from the sluice room.

'Oh no!' Eleanor gasped.

'Poor little mucker has only one sucker to grind his teeth upon!'

Eleanor felt herself flush with anger and embarrassment. She strode over to the sluice room, leaving an appalled-looking Bishop at the ward door. As she walked, Lady Peters' gaze drilled into her back.

She opened the sluice room door. Frank Harrison gazed up at her from his seat by the butler sink. The whole place stank of methylated spirits. He waved a bottle at her. 'You joining the party, Miss?' he said amiably. 'Well that's good.' He stood up, clutching his nightshirt to his privates. Eleanor gaped at him. ''Cos there's a shortage of women in this bloody place.' Eleanor started to close the door, but it was too late. ''Ere, 'ang on,' he said, grabbing hold of it.

He stumbled out into the ward. Lady Peters and the Bishop watched him with bemusement and shock.

Frank squinted at the Bishop, registering only his long robes. 'Shit!' he said to Eleanor, and whistled. 'She's nothing to look at, but I'll give it a go.' He lurched forwards, smiling. 'Hello,' he said.

Eleanor smiled weakly at the Bishop.

There was really nothing left to do but to see the Bishop out, which Lady Peters did while Eleanor instructed Nurse Carr and Daniel to discharge Frank. That done, she went to the street door.

Lady Peters was talking to the Bishop, but he was already

110

in his carriage, and it was clear there was no hope. He rapped on the ceiling to tell the driver to go. Lady Peters marched back to Eleanor. She was in a fury.

'He was only celebrating his operation,' Eleanor said sadly.

Lady Peters was having none of it. 'Well, now he can celebrate losing us the Bishop's Sunday fund.' She stalked inside.

Eleanor followed her. Nurse Carr and Daniel were manhandling Frank Harrison to the door. He was still drunk, but now he was aggressive with it. 'Where you taking me now, you old bat?' he demanded.

Polly, stumbling after with her hat in her hand, giggled.

'You're on the mend now,' Nurse Carr said primly. 'You'll do just as well at home.'

'Recover?' Frank said as if it were an insult. 'I'm in so much pain I'd be better off with me hernia.'

Daniel shoved him hard. 'Doctor Bramwell saved your miserable life, you oaf.'

Frank clutched at Polly and they lurched out into the street together, leaving behind them only the reek of rotgut spirits.

Lady Peters took up a position in front of the consulting room door. 'So this is the colour, life and smell of the East End, is it?' she demanded. 'Well, as far as I'm concerned, the colour is lurid, the life low and the smell is…indescribable.' She turned and stalked into the treatment room.

Eleanor smiled ruefully at Doctor Marsham. There was no denying Lady Peters had a point, at least about the smell. Daniel and Nurse Carr looked at each other, evidently embarrassed, then hurried off about their work. Eleanor and Doctor Marsham shut the outer doors.

'So that's it,' Doctor Marsham said. Eleanor suddenly realized that he'd had at least as much at stake as she did. 'No money, no anaesthesia, no surgery.' He sighed. 'No Doctor Marsham.'

'There are other charities,' Eleanor said as it dawned on her that without him she could not operate either – and then, with a jolt, that she was being selfish. The Thrift was just as much Doctor Marsham's way out of the East London as it had been hers. 'You must think me a fool for allowing this to happen,' she said, trying to soften it.

'Not quite,' he put in.

'But this place is for people like him.' She grew more heated. 'Exactly like him.'

'Then this is just your first battle of many,' Doctor Marsham said.

He is on my side, Eleanor thought. Perhaps he always has been. As if in confirmation, he added, 'I hope you win some of them.'

Eleanor smiled. Before she could say anything, the door of the treatment room banged open and Lady Peters came out. 'Mr Bentley,' she called. Daniel turned round from the hearth, where he was making up the fire. 'Take down that list of regulations.' She glanced sharply at Eleanor. 'And add "no singing at any time".' She turned and disappeared back into the treatment room.

'I'd better go,' Eleanor said. 'We'll talk again later.'

She went into the treatment room and found Lady Peters putting on her jacket, ready to go. Eleanor perched against one of the work benches.

'I'm sorry about the outcome, and for not handling him

better,' Eleanor said. Lady Peters did not look at her, but started pulling on her gloves while staring fixedly at the window. 'But I won't apologize for admitting Mr Harrison.' The stony silence went unbroken. 'How can I?' Eleanor asked.

At last Lady Peters spoke. 'And if three Mr Harrisons come barging in tomorrow?'

Eleanor grinned. She couldn't help it. 'We may need to send out for some more ether.' Lady Peters glared at her without smiling, but there was the tiniest softening of her expression. 'People don't come to us because they love us,' Eleanor said gently. 'They come because it's us or the mortuary.' A thought occurred to her. 'Would you really have sent Frank Harrison to lie on the slab?'

'He cost us a hundred pounds!' Lady Peters said, clearly at the end of her patience. Eleanor stared at her, wondering how you could measure out a man's life in pounds, shillings and pence, or say that because a man drank his life was not worth saving. 'We share the same good intentions, Eleanor,' Lady Peters said, 'but there are ways of doing things.'

Yes, Eleanor thought, and yours would demand that the poor pay with piety and prayers if they cannot with silver and copper. It was not a view she could share. She stared levelly at Lady Peters, who said, 'Oh very well! The minor clergy of Islington, I'll set about wooing them.'

Relief flooded through Eleanor. 'Thank you,' she said. She bent to kiss the older woman's cheek. 'Just say when you want me to dance attendance.'

'Thank you, Eleanor,' Lady Peters said. She smiled ruefully. 'But I think not.'

Eleanor watched her go, then got her own jacket. She supposed she really should go home and check on Miss Heart. Father would be quite desperate by now, if his mood this morning had been indicative, though how he could have feelings for a woman like that, a woman who was no better than she might be and who was intent on drinking herself to death… She paused with her jacket still in her hand.

Frank Harrison was no different. She had treated him happily enough, would have defended her actions to a hundred, a thousand bishops, if it cost them the Sunday funds of every single one.

The only difference between Frank Harrison and Miss Heart was that she held Father's affections, which to Eleanor's mind should have belonged only to her mother. She wiped the back of her hand across her eyes, and it came away wet.

***

She found her father in the guest bedroom. Alone. The bed had been stripped. He was looking wistfully out of the window.

'When did she go?' Eleanor asked softly. He turned and she realized he had not heard her come in. He shrugged and there was such pain on his face that she could not bear to see it, nor to think that she had helped to put it there. 'Don't worry,' she said, 'she'll do whatever's necessary to recover.' She went and leaned against the post at the foot of the bed.

'Give up her theatre?' Father whispered. 'She comes alive on stage. But take her away from it…' his voice trailed off. They both knew the outcome was inevitable.

'I'm very sorry, Father,' Eleanor murmured. She could not look at him.

114

He gave a sad little smile. 'So you should be,' he said severely. 'It's one thing misdiagnosing a charity case, but when you've been paid five shillings…' he added with a ghost of his old mischief.

'I didn't realize she meant so much to you,' Eleanor said, wondering as she said it whether it would be better to leave the subject alone now.

But it was too late. 'Neither did I,' Father said. He stared at the bed. 'I don't suppose I shall see her again.' His mouth tightened, but in pain, not anger. 'You expect too much of people, Eleanor.'

Eleanor swallowed. What she had to say came hard to her. 'I judged her very harshly and with not much thought,' she admitted. She wanted to say, will it help if I go after her – beg her to come back to you? She wanted to turn back time and change what she had done. But the one was as impossible as the other.

'It's not only the poor and dirty that need compassion.'

'No,' Eleanor agreed. Her father looked away. There was nothing she could do but offer him her company through the long evening. 'A medicinal draught then, Father?' She tried to keep her tone light, and almost succeeded. 'A small whisky?'

Father walked over to her. 'Well, I'm feeling very weak, Eleanor,' he said. He covered her hand with his own. 'I think a small one might be a mistake, don't you?'

Together, they went down to the drawing room.

Chapter 10

Golden summer gave way to mellow autumn, and autumn to a biting winter. As the seasons changed, Lady Peters finally secured funding for Doctor Marsham and an assistant for Nurse Carr. Daniel was fitted with a peg and a shoe, and learned to hobble on it with the aid of a walking stick. The Thrift was never empty, and often full to overflowing. Eleanor had never been happier.

***

Eleanor was preparing to go home from the Thrift. Nurse Carr was still doing the week's washing, but there was no-one in the waiting room and Eleanor had decided that this once she could allow herself to leave just a little early. It was, after all, her birthday, and her father had, as usual, arranged a small party for her. She started to say goodnight to Nurse Carr but just then there was a clamour at the door.

She turned to see two men in Lady Peters' household livery carrying in a very young, very pregnant girl. Lady Peters herself stood by the door, biting her lip in consternation. The girl let out a long moan. She was dressed in a coarse, plain skirt and blouse, and her hair draggled over her face. Her breath came in long, ragged gasps.

'Eleanor,' Lady Peters called. 'Eleanor, she's in a dreadful state.' Eleanor hurried over. 'There,' Lady Peters said to the girl. 'You'll be looked after now.' Eleanor ushered the men through to the treatment room.

The girl moaned again. 'It's too early,' she said to no-one in particular. Her face looked flushed. 'It isn't due for weeks.'

'Thank you,' Eleanor said to Lady Peters. 'We'll take her.'

The men laid the girl on the table. She was crying continuously now. 'It's too soon, Miss,' she said through her sobs. 'It shouldn't be coming yet.' She was clearly in pain...

'They come when they're ready, not when you are,' Nurse Carr said briskly. She went to get sheets for a bed in the ward.

And then just as clearly the pain stopped. Contractions, then, Eleanor thought. That might be bad, or very bad.

She got her stethoscope. 'Try to stop crying,' she said, no more gently. 'It doesn't help.'

'If every woman made this fuss...' Nurse Carr said, piling the sheets up onto Daniel's outstretched arms.

He hobbled off.

Eleanor bent to listen to the baby's heart. Outside, she heard Lady Peters say to Daniel, 'Apparently, she's been my laundry woman for nearly a year. Why she kept working in her condition, I don't know.'

'Ah well, they get it into their heads that they need luxuries like bread and that,' Daniel replied. Then he walked off, his peg making a distinctive clumping sound as he went.

Eleanor smiled. She could just imagine the expression on Lady Peters' face; but then she forced herself to concentrate and was rewarded with the distinctive rapid patter of a foetal heartbeat. She took the examination further. 'What's your name?' she asked, to distract the girl while she palpated her abdomen.

'Clare, Miss,' the girl said. Her sobs had subsided. 'Clare…' There was the slightest hesitation. 'Carter, Miss.'

Eleanor examined her cervix, having first to wipe away some blood. That was worrying, and it looked as though the baby might not be presenting properly. But there had been no more contractions, so with luck it would be a problem for another day – and perhaps by then the problem would have righted itself.

She went off to wash her hands while Nurse Carr cleaned Clare and got her sitting up.

'You belong at home with your family,' Nurse Carr said as Eleanor came back, drying her hands.

'I've got none,' Clare protested. 'I was chucked out months ago.'

Eleanor stared down at her. Unmarried, no doubt, and no better than she should be. 'I'd say you're about a month early,' she said, 'but that's not too terrible.'

'If you'd stop all that crying and carrying on, you'd feel better,' Nurse Carr said as she took the bloody towels over to the wash basket.

'Now, you've had a small bleed so I'm going to keep you in tonight, where we can keep an eye on you,' Eleanor said. Whatever she might think of Clare Carter's morals, she wasn't about to dismiss her medical problems because of her: she'd learned that from Peggy Heart, if nothing else. Clare looked dolefully up at her. 'The contractions have stopped so you could carry this baby to term,' Eleanor said, 'and that's better for both of you.' She glanced up at Nurse Carr. 'We'd better send a message to the father.'

'He can't come,' Clare said quickly.

'Is he at work?' Eleanor asked. Clare looked away; she had been right then, Eleanor thought: the girl was clearly not married. 'Do you want us to let him know where you are, at least?'

'No,' Clare said. She smiled and her plain face was transformed. 'He's at sea,' she said proudly. 'He's a sailor.' She turned round to Nurse Carr. 'He's on a boat,' she added, as if they might not have worked this out. She slumped suddenly. 'Miss?' she asked. 'Is it normal? The baby?' She nodded at the stethoscope. 'Can you tell with that thing?'

'I can hear your heart and the baby's with this, and they're both normal,' Eleanor reassured her. Clare still didn't look quite convinced but perhaps only time would do that. Eleanor went on, 'Nurse Carr will put you to bed, and…'

'Doctor?' Daniel said from the doorway.

Eleanor bit her lip. 'Oh!' she said. 'I know – my father's sent the carriage.' Tonight of all nights it wouldn't do to be late. She hurried over to the peg to get her hat and coat. 'I'm just coming.'

'No, it's her…' Daniel said in an undertone, as if he could avoid Clare hearing. 'It's her old man. He's outside.'

'Not my old man, Miss,' Clare protested, perhaps too quickly. 'It can't be mine – he's at sea.'

'He ain't now,' Daniel insisted. 'He's outside.'

Eleanor frowned. 'Then show him in,' Eleanor said, puzzled. She finished buttoning her coat.

'He shouldn't be here,' Clare wailed.

Daniel looked embarrassed. 'I didn't like…' his voice trailed off. 'He's a bit…you might not like him.'

'For goodness' sake,' Eleanor said, picking up her hat. 'Whether I like him is neither here nor there.'

She swept past him into the waiting room, only to be brought up short when she saw the man standing there. His skin was the colour of chocolate and his hair was frizzy and jet black; but he was clean enough, in a frayed cloth jacket, with a neckerchief knotted round his throat and a battered cap on his head.

Eleanor had only ever seen a Negro once before. She stared at him, wondering what he was doing there. He was obviously not ill.

'Sorry, Miss,' he said. His voice was surprisingly ordinary. 'Can I see my wife?' He fiddled with his glove, pulling it part-way off and then putting it back on again.

'We don't have your wife,' Eleanor said. There was obviously some mistake.

'I went to where she works and they told me that she was here,' he insisted. 'Gone into labour.'

'But…' Eleanor glanced back at the treatment room. 'This woman's English,' she protested.

The man swallowed. 'Yes, Miss,' he said. 'Clare Carter. Washerwoman.' Eleanor stared at him, bemused. It was no wonder Clare had lied that her man was at sea. 'Is she all right?' he whispered. He was clearly agitated now.

'Yes,' Eleanor said. She licked her lips. She supposed there was nothing to be done about it, so they would just have to do their best, but she had never in her life imagined that such a person would come to the Thrift. 'She's much better…' she started. 'You'd better see her.' She smiled nervously and turned to lead him into the treatment room.

'Charlie!' Clare exclaimed. She sounded alarmed but her eyes said she was pleased to see him. 'You shouldn't have

120

come.' She sat on the examination bench, gripping the edge so hard her knuckles were white. 'Go away,' she pleaded, but he hurried over to her. 'God, what do you think you're doing, coming here?'

He stopped her protestations with a kiss. 'Be quiet,' he said.

Eleanor stared at him, not sure whether or not to be outraged. On the one hand, he obviously didn't know how decent people behaved. On the other he was so obviously worried about his…wife that she couldn't help but be touched. Perhaps, she thought, perhaps it's different where he comes from.

Charlie – so he had an English name, then, Eleanor mused – turned to her and said, 'What's the matter with her, Miss?' as politely as you could wish.

'Not a great deal,' Eleanor answered. 'But she needs peace and quiet, so please don't stay too long.' Charlie nodded. Eleanor turned to go. As she reached the door, she said to Nurse Carr, 'If her labour starts again, just send for me.'

Nurse Carr followed her into the waiting room. 'No wonder she didn't want us seeing him.' Eleanor ignored that. She still had bad memories of her father's face after Peggy Heart had left, and she never again wanted to make the mistake of tempering her medical advice with moral indignation. So she kept her voice neutral and said, 'Hourly checks that she hasn't started bleeding again.'

Nurse Carr bit her lip. 'Do you think he's the father, doctor? I've never delivered a black baby before…'

'I don't suppose many nurses have,' Eleanor said, relieved that there was at least some substance to Nurse Carr's preoccupation. She tried to sound soothing, though in truth she was just as worried as her nurse. 'Anyway,' she said, trying to reassure herself as much as Nurse Carr, 'it's probably a false labour. I doubt if anything will happen.'

She left, hoping it were true.

***

A birthday party was hardly an appropriate place to ask her father about premature labours, but Eleanor had no choice: she was so late home that the guests – six of them, including Lady Peters – had arrived before she had finished dressing.

She wore the pearl choker that had belonged to her mother. It went well with the aqua silk dress she had chosen, and besides, it pleased her father as much as anything could on this one bittersweet night of the year.

And now, she stood asking him about difficult births, knowing what it must cost him to answer, while around them their guests entertained themselves.

'Of course,' he said, 'the birth process is the same, whatever the race or nationality.'

Eleanor wound a loop of her silver chain round her gloved fingers. 'If it's a breech birth – and it looks as though it may well be – will the child be too big for the mother's pelvis?'

'How can I tell?' Father said, clearly exasperated. 'Is she small, this mother?'

Eleanor was taken aback by his reaction: surely he had heard the theory, often expounded in the hospitals, though rarely tested in practice, that a child of…mixed birth…would be larger than normal? But Father was speaking again. 'Not particularly,' she said.

'Well then,' Father said as if there were no difference between this birth and any other. 'There shouldn't be any problem.'

Eleanor tried again. She licked her lips. 'I've never had to intervene in a birth before and...'

'And you probably won't have to this time,' Father cut in. He patted her reassuringly on the arm. 'Now, let's steer this conversation to more genteel topics, shall we?' He walked over to Kate and picked up two glasses of white wine from her tray. Handing one to Eleanor, he said, 'Ladies and gentlemen, before we go in I would like to propose a toast.' He waited a heartbeat for the conversation to stop and then went on, 'To Eleanor, on her birthday – the dearest daughter a man could wish for.' Eleanor smiled, partly in embarrassment, partly in simple pleasure. 'Eleanor,' he said, raising his glass.

'Eleanor!' the guests chorused, Lady Peters foremost among them. They drank.

And then Father turned to Eleanor as he always did and added gravely, as he always did, 'And of course, as always, Eleanor's mother, my dear Mary.'

Eleanor couldn't bear to look at him, at the pain in his eyes. She never could, not on this one night of the year. 'Mother,' she whispered, raising her glass.

'Mary,' the guests said, but they were less jovial now.

'She saw her daughter only once, but she would have been proud tonight,' Father said. He paused. And then the moment passed and he added impishly, 'And exasperated. And appalled.' The guests laughed. So did Eleanor. And then Father's mood switched again and he said, 'But most of all she would have loved you. To distraction.' Eleanor smiled at him. What else could she do, when she could see his heart breaking in front of her? How it must have been that night...

'And you're so like her,' Lady Peters said loudly. She turned to the rest of the guests. 'Two peas in a pod!'

Once Eleanor would have been appalled at Lady Peters' terrible timing. Now she wasn't so sure – someone had had to break the mood, or they would have been maudlin all night.

Father must have felt it too. 'Dinner,' he said.

The food, of course, was delicious, the company amusing, and Eleanor managed to put aside her worries until the dessert was served. Then Kate hurried in, leaving the door ajar behind her. Eleanor glanced at her and saw first the note in her hand and then Daniel Bentley standing in the hall. Her stomach turned to ice, and she did not need to read Nurse Carr's badly spelled but beautifully penned note to know that Clare Carter had gone into labour.

'If you'll excuse me?' she said to the guests on either side of her, and went round the table to talk to her father.

'It's definitely breech,' she said without preamble. It was obvious from his expression that he'd come to the correct conclusion about the provenance of the note. His face was set like stone. 'A month premature, Father,' she added, hoping to soften him.

'You have guests,' he said. 'You'll have to call Doctor Marsham.'

Eleanor shook her head. 'He's away for the week. His father's ill.'

'No!' Father said, as loudly as if they'd been alone.

'I can't do it all on my own. My first difficult birth.' Eleanor's tone was as loud. She was beginning to panic. Her pulse was racing. The guests continued talking but they couldn't have helped overhearing. She added, more quietly,

'She's had a small bleed, Father.'

His mouth quirked impatiently. 'Haven't you got a nurse there?'

'It may well be placenta praevia…'

'Oh for God's sake,' Father said, clearly furious.

But so was Eleanor, now. 'You can't let a mother and child die because it's tonight rather than tomorrow night.' His eyes went wide with pain and shock. She went on anyway. 'Or tomorrow night.'

He threw down his napkin. 'Eleanor!' he shouted.

'I didn't plan it, Father.' She felt the blood burn in her cheeks. 'We can hardly let her die because she's chosen the wrong day.'

He stood up. 'Now that's enough.' He glared at her.

She refused to look away, though she was suddenly aware that all the guests were listening and doubtless had been for some time.

'I need your help,' she said. She was begging now. She didn't care.

Father turned to the guests. 'Ladies and gentlemen,' he blustered. 'What can I say?'

Say you'll help, only that you'll help, Eleanor thought; but she knew she had already won.

'Why,' Lady Peters said, 'you can say it's all my fault for taking her to the Thrift in the first place.' Her smile lit up her face. There was a scattering of laughter. She leaned across the table and patted his hand. 'I'll look after everyone, don't worry.'

That's that then, Eleanor thought with satisfaction. Father might ignore her pleas but he could never resist Lady Peters.

Then again, Eleanor had yet to meet the man who could.

'Well, if only she were the washerwoman,' Father said, attempting lightness but not quite achieving it, 'and some other fool had let his daughter go into doctoring…' It was quite the worst joke Eleanor had ever heard him make. He nodded to the guests. 'Excuse me,' he said.

Chapter 11

Clare screamed. Eleanor heard her while she was still in the street. Daniel pressed the keys into her half-frozen fingers, and she fumbled open the door of the Thrift, while behind her the carriage clattered off. Her breath hung in the air, and then she had the door open and a burst of light and warmth greeted her.

Through the internal windows of the treatment room she could see Nurse Carr and her assistant scurrying around, while the unmistakable bulk of Clare Carter thrashed around on the table.

Eleanor hurried inside, with her father close behind her and Daniel bringing up the rear.

There was a red bloodstain on the sheet covering Clare. Eleanor glanced at it, then at the tray of knives on the trolley near the foot of the bed.

'With her losing blood, I thought I'd better set up for all eventualities,' Nurse Carr said, carrying in a stack of towels from the linen cupboard.

Eleanor stripped off her coat and dumped it on the side. As she grabbed her apron she said, 'We're just fortunate you were still here.'

Father had drawn back Clare's nightgown, and was palpating her abdomen. He looked grim.

Clare's breath was coming in gasps.

Eleanor covered the distance to her side in two strides, grabbing a pinnard from the trolley as she went. She hadn't had time to collect her medical bag with her stethoscope and other instruments before she left.

'Someone help her...' said a voice from behind her. Charlie, she thought. 'Please,' he begged. He went round and stood by Clare's head. He reached out to touch her but didn't quite dare.

Eleanor didn't have time to be irritated that he was there. She put the pinnard to Clare's abdomen and listened to the baby's heart. She glanced at her father. He was looking under the blanket. 'The baby's heart is racing,' she said.

He nodded and held up a blood-soaked towel. 'The blood loss is bad,' he said.

'Someone help her,' Charlie demanded. Eleanor glanced at him. His hands were pressed together as if he were praying. Perhaps some missionary had taught him how.

'We have to do a Caesarean, Father,' Eleanor said.

He nodded and took the pinnard from her.

Eleanor turned to Clare. 'We're going to help the baby on its way,' she said, but the girl's eyes were bright with pain and there was no telling if she understood. Her skin was ashen – almost blue – and slick with sweat.

Father stood up. 'The sooner the better,' he said.

Nurse Carr held up a fresh apron. 'Out you go,' she said over her shoulder to Charlie.

'I'm not leaving her,' he protested. He was clearly panicking.

He wasn't the only one. 'Get him out!' Eleanor

commanded as Nurse Carr tied her apron strings.

Daniel chivvied Charlie. 'Out you go,' he said, forcing back the other man.

Charlie tried to dodge round him. His eyes were huge in his dark face. 'What's wrong with her?' he asked. He glanced at the trolley with its array of scalpels, specula and retractors, and tried again to dodge round Daniel. 'I mean, what are you going to do to her?'

Save her, Eleanor thought as she started to wash her hands. Dear God, please let me.

'None of your business, son,' Daniel said. He shoved the man out of the door. 'Leave it to the doctors.'

'Now,' Father said, as Nurse Carr looped an apron over his head. 'She'll be quite safe.'

It was clear from his face that he didn't believe it. He made a tutting noise. Eleanor looked round to see that he had just passed the tray of instruments. He came over to the sink.

He pulled off his wedding ring – his wedding ring, Eleanor thought, and wondered what this must be costing him – and started to roll up his sleeves.

'God, please tell me this is some jolly jape,' he said so quietly only Eleanor could possibly hear him. 'I presume that in a minute you'll wheel out the proper instruments and you'll be shouting "April fool!" ' He turned to wash his hands.

Eleanor stared at him. She knew his bitter humour was just his way of defending himself, but she couldn't bring herself to appreciate it just now, much less join in. 'Father, we have no time for this,' she said.

'This place is no more suitable for major surgery than a stables.' He wasn't joking now. He started to dry his hands.

'The lighting is dreadful, the table's completely unsuitable…'

Clare began to scream.

'Lie still,' Nurse Carr pleaded with her. 'There's a good girl…'

Eleanor and her father rushed over to her.

'I can't breathe,' she gasped. 'I can't…' She tried to sit up but failed. Her shoulders slammed back into the table.

'Check the bleed, Nurse,' Eleanor shouted.

Her father tried to restrain Clare but the girl was thrashing around. Eleanor tried to help him. Clare's skin looked waxy but it was ice cold to the touch. 'She's very cold, Father,' Eleanor said, and realized that neither of them could do anything while they were occupied with holding her down. 'Mr Bentley!' she shouted. 'Mr Bentley!'

Nurse Carr tried to look under the end blanket but Clare's flailing legs stopped her getting close. There was hardly any need, anyway – the whole lower part of the bed was soaked with blood.

'Stop fighting us,' Nurse Carr pleaded, despairingly.

'She can't hear you,' Eleanor said to her; and to her father, 'Her brain is starved of oxygen.' That would be the blood loss. If they didn't do something soon, there'd be no point in doing anything at all.

Clare's body convulsed again. An animal howl came out of her throat. Her arms and legs flailed spastically. Her foot narrowly missed Nurse Carr but caught the equipment trolley. Instruments flew all over the floor, most landing in the great puddle of blood at the base of the bed. As the night nurse started to pick them up, Daniel Bentley arrived.

'I'll hold her,' he said, pushing down on her shoulders.

'Damn it. She's bleeding to death,' Father said. 'We'll have to knock her out.'

'Ether?' Eleanor asked. Behind Father, the night nurse was clumsily righting the instrument trolley. Clare whimpered. Her movements were getting weaker.

'Too slow,' Father said. 'Chloroform – quick!'

Eleanor raced to the cupboard for the bottle. She unscrewed it and poured chloroform onto the towel Father held out. He held it over Clare's face. Eleanor could see in his face the effort he was making to be gentle as she struggled against him and Mr Bentley. Her head thrashed from side to side and she coughed. Her hands clawed the air. Then suddenly she went quiet.

Father took the towel away from her face. He nodded to Eleanor.

'Get her ready,' she said to the nurses.

'Look at these,' Nurse Carr said, holding up a jug containing the instruments, which were bloodied from falling on the floor. 'We haven't got any more.'

'Well bloody well boil them again, for God's sake,' Father snapped.

Nurse Carr looked shocked. 'Replace those you can, boil the others,' Eleanor said more gently. The last thing she needed was Nurse Carr going off in one of her sulks. 'Clean up the worst of the blood,' she added to the night nurse.

She poured antiseptic into an enamel kidney dish. Out of the corner of her eye she saw her father palpate Clare's abdomen. He stood up and put his fingers against the girl's neck. She could see from the tightness of his mouth that something was wrong.

'She's failing,' he said. He shut his eyes, concentrating on what his fingers told him. 'Pulse is thready…' he muttered. He bent and put his cheek to her face.

No, Eleanor thought. Please God, not this. Not tonight…

'She's stopped breathing,' her father said.

'I'll get a stimulant,' Eleanor said. 'We've got strychnine.'

'Too slow,' Father contradicted her. He looked round wildly, obviously trying to see what else they had. 'Ether,' he commanded. Eleanor passed him the bottle. 'Try to shock her out of it.' He unstoppered the bottle. 'Stand back.'

Eleanor moved away. He splashed ether on Clare's chest. She gasped. Her eyes went wide with shock and her whole body arced into rigidity. Then she slumped back against the table. And rasped out a breath. Once, twice and again.

Thank God, Eleanor thought. Thank…

And then there was silence.

No! Eleanor thought. Her father snatched up his stethoscope. He pulled Clare's nightgown away from her chest and pressed the end of the instrument against her skin.

'Come on,' he urged. 'Come on.' He moved the instrument to her neck, but the answer was written on his face. 'Nothing,' he said. He pulled off the stethoscope. After a moment, he stood up. Eleanor touched his arm gently. 'It's too late,' he said. The grief in his eyes was terrible to see.

'She was so frightened,' Eleanor murmured. 'Poor girl.' She would not, dare not, think of that night twenty-seven years ago when her mother had been just as frightened, and her father's eyes as full of grief.

'But the child's still alive,' Father said suddenly. 'Caesarean, Eleanor.' She nodded, astonished that in the midst of his own pain he could think so quickly and compassionately. 'We'll have to be quick.'

'I'll get the clean instruments,' Nurse Carr said, moving off without waiting to be told.

'No time. No point,' Father said. He turned back to Eleanor. 'Eleanor, agree she's dead.'

Eleanor bent and listened for heartbeat. Nothing. 'She's dead.'

'Scalpel,' Father said. She turned and rummaged in the tray. 'Any scalpel, please,' Father said. Nurse Carr hurried over to help her. 'For once we don't have to worry about the size of the incision.' Eleanor handed him a knife, and he drew a bloody line down Clare's abdomen. 'Retractors,' he demanded. Eleanor inserted the retractors, but however hard she pulled on them the muscle tried to pull back. 'That's it,' Father said. 'More. Come on, you can't hurt her now.' Eleanor strained and at last the cavity opened. 'Let's at least save this wretched child,' Father said. Eleanor struggled with the retractors. 'You take over from her,' Father called to Daniel, who came and took the instruments out of her hands, though he looked terribly nauseous. Eleanor stepped back. 'Put your back into it,' Father ordered. He glanced up. 'Eleanor, you stand back for the child.'

'A towel for the baby,' Eleanor said to the night nurse. She hurried round to Father's other side. He dabbed blood out of the way, then threw the swab on the floor. Then he cut carefully into the uterus. He pulled back the membranes...and there was the baby, perfectly formed but the wrong way round.

'Shall I take it?' Eleanor asked.

Father nodded, a huge, exhausted movement. 'In you go,' he said. And then, 'Damn it, the placenta's in the way.' Eleanor

133

stopped. 'Can anything else bloody well go wrong here?' he demanded. He grabbed a knife and hacked at it until the baby was free.

Eleanor took the baby gently out of its – her, Eleanor saw now – mother's dead womb. She was covered in mucus but was beautiful in the way of tiny babies.

Eleanor slapped her on the bottom, and she howled in outrage. It was, Eleanor thought, the smallest of many hurts her life was likely to bring.

Nurse Carr handed Eleanor a towel and together they cleaned the baby, then tied off the umbilicus.

'I'd better tell the father,' Nurse Carr said unwillingly.

'No,' Eleanor said. She sighed. 'I'll do it.'

Chapter 12

Charlie smiled at Eleanor. She walked slowly towards him, cradling his baby in her arms. Slowly, because he was delighted, and she didn't want to take that from him. She stopped in front of him. He reached down and moved the blanket aside, then touched the child's cheek: his huge finger, dark against her coffee-coloured skin. The baby grizzled softly to herself.

'Your daughter,' Eleanor murmured. 'She's perfect.' But she thought, just another moment of happiness and he'll realize.

He nodded to her. Swallowed. His eyes were glassy with tears. It was a terrible thing, to Eleanor, to see a grown man cry.

'I'm so sorry,' Eleanor said.

He looked as if his heart would break. Had broken. Eleanor turned away to leave him with his grief. She went into the treatment room. After a moment she heard him trudge after her.

She tried not to watch him, but she couldn't help herself. He took the baby and went to the table where Clare lay. Nurse Carr had covered her with a sheet to hide the butchery they had done to her.

Charlie stood for a moment by the table. His jaw worked as he looked at Clare's bloodless face. He drew in a long, ragged breath.

Then he bent down and held the baby up to Clare, as if to let her see the child. Perhaps he thinks she really can, Eleanor thought. She had heard that Africans believed in ghosts, in spirits; perhaps he were right.

If God is good, she found herself thinking fiercely, then that poor girl does know she has a daughter. She does. It was what her maternal grandmother used to say to her, when she was tiny.

Or perhaps Charlie didn't believe it, or got no comfort from it: he was crying properly now, huge body-wracking sobs he hardly tried to conceal.

A noise drew Eleanor's attention from him. She saw that her father was watching too. He was holding his wedding ring in his hand, turning it over and over while he stared at Charlie. Abruptly, he got up and went into the kitchen. Eleanor followed him.

She found him sitting in the half-dark, still staring at his hands. 'I'm so sorry, Father,' she whispered. 'That must have brought back terrible memories.' She found her own eyes were pricking with tears.

'Yes,' he said. He sat up a little straighter. 'Yes it did.' His breathing came hard and ragged. 'Very bad memories.' There was nothing mischievous in him now, nothing of Lady Peters' grand old pirate. 'But not', he added after a long, silent moment, 'as bad as what we've just had to do in there.'

He was blaming her, Eleanor realized with horror. He had never blamed her for her mother's death, though many men might have. 'My infirmary did, after all, save the child,' she said stiffly.

Father launched himself out of his chair and strode across the room, as if action could dissipate anger and grief. 'It was more by good luck than management,' he said, clearly exasperated with her. 'Good God,' he went on, 'that operating equipment's barbaric.' He started to fumble with his cuffs. 'I've seen better on the battlefield.' His voice was thick with tears and he couldn't quite manage his cufflinks. 'A world which I thought I'd left behind.'

Eleanor went to him then. He held up his hand for her to help him. She could feel him shaking, feel him trying to breathe easily, trying not to cry.

She would have said something, but whatever it was might have sounded like pity, and she knew he could not have borne that.

***

A little later, when they were both more composed, they faced Charlie. He had, Nurse Carr grumbled, refused to give up the child even long enough for her to be washed, nor could he see that he needed help to look after her.

He sat in the waiting room, rocking back and forth, back and forth as he held the baby. She made desperate little kitten noises in her hunger.

Eleanor brushed back a strand of errant hair from her forehead. 'Mr Carter,' she said, 'Nurse Carr knows a wet nurse, which may solve your first problem.' He stared at her, dull-eyed. Eleanor glanced at Nurse Carr and sighed heavily. 'To foster her until she's weaned,' she explained. Daniel had already gone to fetch the woman. There was no other way.

Charlie didn't answer. He just looked at the child. Nurse Carr tried to take her from him but he put his arm up as if to defend her. 'I'll find a wet nurse at home,' he said.

Eleanor glanced at her father, suddenly feeling the weight of all her exhaustion coming down on her. 'She's not well enough to go home,' she said, striving to keep her voice gentle, her manner non-threatening.

'She hasn't even been washed yet,' Nurse Carr added more sharply.

Charlie looked from one to the other. Eleanor wondered if he even understood what they were saying.

'Her lungs are weak,' Father said, as he'd already said before. He sounded tired but there was no sign of the emotion that had debilitated him not twenty minutes earlier. 'She's very small – she needs nursing, for Heaven's sake!'

'I'm going,' Charlie said. He stood up. 'Taking her.'

Eleanor glared up at him and for all his height, she snapped, 'You will not take that child out of this building.' At least he didn't try to move away. There was panic in his eyes. Despair. Eleanor softened. 'For the child's sake,' she added, almost pleading.

Charlie stared at her for a long moment more. He licked his lips, then nodded, fractionally. Nurse Carr took the baby from him. He watched her as she walked away.

His tongue worked over his lips. 'I don't know what to do,' he said. He sat back down. 'We thought that she would be so big…'

'She was born too soon,' Eleanor said. 'She's tiny.' She didn't know what to say to him in his grief.

'It's my fault,' he said. She saw something come into his expression then – the beginnings of guilt that, left to harden, would blight everything he did, every day of his life.

Again, she didn't know how to deal with it.

Her father stepped forward. 'Loss of blood killed your wife, not the child,' he said gently. Eleanor looked at him, wondering how many men in England would have been able to say that with such compassion to a man like Charlie, whom some would have treated no better than a dog. She felt a surge of pride. 'You have to accept that,' Father went on. 'If you don't, you'll go mad.'

Eleanor wondered who had said that to him when she had been born, and how many times he had repeated it to himself before he had believed it.

'I don't know what to do,' Charlie said again, as if he were confiding a great secret.

'You go home,' Father said. 'That's all you can do. Try to get some sleep,' he finished, as if Charlie were any of his paying patients. Before anyone could say anything else, he walked away. 'Don't be long, Eleanor,' he said as he went out the door.

Eleanor smiled wearily at his retreating back then went and started to clear out a drawer to use as a cradle. Nurse Carr came to help her and together they made it as comfortable for the child as they could, with cut-down blankets and half a sheet.

Nurse Carr put the baby to bed while Eleanor fetched her jacket. She was suddenly freezing, not only with the cold of the night but also with tiredness.

As she came back into the ward, the front door rattled open. Daniel came in, accompanied by a scruffy little sparrow of a woman, who must be Martha Green, the wet nurse. Her voice preceded her.

'I'll need paying for each feed as we go along. I don't give milk for nothing,' she said. Her feet pattered on the floor and she clutched a shawl round her thin shoulders. 'Got to feed myself to make milk, when all's said and done,' she went on as they came through the glass doors into the ward. 'No good thinking it comes cheap, because it doesn't.' She glared up at Nurse Carr, as if some great injustice had already been done to her. 'People think it's free,' she rattled on. 'I say, I don't live for free.' She smelled faintly of gin. She pulled back the blanket from the baby. 'Oh my God,' she exclaimed.

She stood up and glared at Nurse Carr, who glared back at her primly.

'The child is two hours old and premature,' Eleanor said.

'Black as the night,' Mrs Green said, as if it were a personal affront.

Eleanor ignored her tone. 'If you would agree to six feeds a day.'

'Feeds? Me?' Mrs Green said. 'My English milk for this little heathen?' She turned to Nurse Carr. 'Well, Ethel Carr, if this is the sort of thing you call me out for,' she turned and marched out even faster than she had come in.

Eleanor darted ahead of her. Out of the corner of her eye, she saw Charlie sitting with his shoulders slumped and resignation on his face. This is what he's used to, she thought. It enraged her. He'd so clearly loved his wife, and as clearly loved his child. And she herself had come so close to dismissing him... No-one else was going to die in her infirmary that night: not just for the want of English milk. 'Don't just walk out,' she said, and got in front of Mrs Green, forcing her to a standstill. 'We've spent half the night

140

saving this child's life, and we're not going to let her starve to death now.'

'Get one of her own kind in then,' Mrs Green snapped with sullen defiance.

'She's hungry and you're not,' Eleanor pointed out.

'I'm not staying,' said Martha Green and made to go.

Eleanor pulled herself up to her full height. 'Sit down,' she commanded. 'Right there.' She pointed to one of the benches. 'Nurse Carr, prepare a trolley to express some of this woman's milk.'

'I won't!'

'Nine pence,' Eleanor said. She could probably have bullied the woman into giving one feed but she needed to be sure she would come back; and where Mrs Green seemed lacking in maternal instinct, her baser ones all seemed intact.

She looked at Eleanor slyly. 'A feed?' she asked.

'A day,' Nurse Carr intoned, before Eleanor could answer.

Good old Nurse Carr, she thought. Eleanor had had no idea what the going rate was, though four shillings and sixpence a day did seem rather a lot. Exasperated by the woman's greed and lack of compassion, she said, 'We're not asking you to suckle the child, just come here four times a day and use the bottles we'll have ready for you.'

Mrs Green sniffed. She pulled her shawl round her and went and sat down, in exactly the place Eleanor had indicated.

Eleanor went past her into the ward. Charlie was still sitting where she had left him. She stifled her irritation and said, 'Mr Carter, your wife's body will be sent to the mortuary in the morning.' She really didn't want to go home with him still there. Grief-stricken as he was, she wasn't sure what he

141

might do and it didn't seem fair to leave Nurse Carr to deal with him, even with Daniel to help her. 'Now the child needs feeding and it's time you went home.'

She went into the treatment room, hoping he would do as he was told; but she didn't hear him leave.

Daniel was mopping up blood from around the table. He was as pale with tiredness as the rest of the staff. 'Would you bring in some screens, please, Mr Bentley?' He nodded and hobbled off to get them.

Clare's dead, white face stared up at the ceiling. Eleanor pulled the sheet over her. She paused for a moment. It was hardly the first dead body she had ever seen. Just the one that had cost her the most.

She was so tired she could have wept: wept for Clare and Charlie who must do without her now; wept for the child, who would probably grow up without either of them, a workhouse brat; wept for her father, remembering what he had tried so hard to forget. But most of all, wept for herself, who had never known a mother's loving touch. She sighed, and forced back the wave of self-pity that was so close to engulfing her.

There was one more thing to do. One more, and she could go home and sleep. She went to her desk and took out the cashbox. Nine pence a day. She started to count out the coppers.

A shadow fell over the desk. She looked up and saw Charlie standing in the doorway. Startled, she slammed the cashbox shut and shoved it in the drawer, out of sight. They stared at each other for a long while. The look in his eyes was the same as it had been when Martha Green had refused to suckle the baby. Worse. He'd come to think he might trust her.

'Your nurse thought I would steal food while my wife was dying,' Charlie said. He, too, sounded tired enough to weep.

'I'm sorry,' Eleanor said. 'I wasn't thinking.' No, she thought at herself as she got out the cashbox again. You were just reacting. She started to count Mrs Green's money again. He's different from us, so he must be wicked.

'Put it away,' he said. 'I've paid her.' He started to put his jacket on. 'I feed my own family.'

That surprised Eleanor. She hadn't expected him to have money. 'Of course,' she said, trying to sound as if she meant it. She slammed the cashbox shut. 'Good.'

'You won't do nothing with the child?' he asked. Eleanor looked at him questioningly. 'Put her out to a workhouse or anything?'

Eleanor paused from putting the box away. 'While she needs to be here, this is where she'll stay.' She knew that others would argue differently, but for the moment it was the truth. 'We won't be putting her out anywhere.' She couldn't help sounding a little indignant.

Charlie looked contrite. All the anger drained from his face. 'I'm sorry,' he said. 'It's just that you get used to being treated like nothing.' Yes, Eleanor thought, by the Martha Greens of this world. Even by me. Only Father had shown him true compassion, and that in the midst of his own pain. 'And if I don't look after her, she got no-one,' he said. His jaw worked against threatening tears. 'Her name, Miss,' he said, 'it's May.'

Eleanor smiled at him sadly. 'You've decided so soon?'

'Clare's choice, Miss.' He looked away from her. 'May for a girl...' His mouth trembled. 'She...' he started, but the words wouldn't come. 'She…' he tried again. 'She wanted a…' he was nearly in tears.

Eleanor couldn't face that much grief, not with exhaustion battering her down. She rubbed her hand across her face. 'I'm sorry, we're all exhausted.' He stared at her. None more exhausted than he, she realized. 'There's nothing more we can do,' she went on, and still he stared at her. Guilt made her voice sharp. 'You have to go home now.'

He nodded at last and turned to go. Eleanor sat alone for a moment in the pool of light cast by the oil lamp on the table. The carriage had long since left. She would have to walk home, but she didn't think she could put one foot in front of the other. Wearily, she got up and found her cape.

***

Eleanor crept into the house as quietly as she could, but the door slipped out of her hand and banged shut. She winced. Just as she took off her cape, the hall clock chimed two o'clock. She started upstairs. Before she got half-way, the silence was pierced by the sound of a single piano note. She stopped in surprise and went back down.

Father was in the parlour. He sat at the piano, with one hand picking out a sad little tune in a minor key. Eleanor went over to him.

'Well, you took your time,' he said without looking round. There was a decanter of whisky at his side and a glass next to it. 'I hope Mr Bentley walked you home.' He picked up the glass and sipped from it.

'Yes,' Eleanor said. 'He did.'

'And the African has gone?' He drained the glass.

'Yes.' He still hadn't looked at her. 'You shouldn't have waited up,' she said.

'What the attraction of that awful place is…'

He was angry, Eleanor realized. At her. At himself. She couldn't cope with it, not after everything. 'Not tonight, Father. Please.'

'What sort of workplace is that for a young woman? Misery…'

Eleanor knew him too well to think he would stop. She got up. 'Good night, Father.' She kissed him on the cheek.

'And poverty.'

'Sleep well.' She went to the door.

'Well, if you are going to throw your life away…' he said heatedly. He paused. She saw his shoulders slump the tiniest bit. 'I'll sort you out some decent equipment.' It was the last thing she had expected. 'There's a set of scalpels, for a start.'

She walked back to him, slowly. 'I didn't know you had any surgical equipment,' she said.

'It's what I was, Eleanor.' It took a moment for her to work out that he wasn't talking about his army days: he meant before Mother had died…before he had failed to save her. He was silent for a long time then, and it was that which told Eleanor she was right. 'You'd better have them,' he said at last.

In that moment she knew – finally knew beyond doubt – that whatever he might say, however he might complain, he accepted her work and her involvement with the Thrift.

Chapter 13

Eleanor barely had time to think about Baby May until the next afternoon, when the Thrift was finally cleared of patients. She sat in the kitchen nursing the child, while outside Nurse Carr hung up to dry the rags they were using for nappies.

Such a tiny thing, Eleanor thought, looking at the child. The bottle was almost as big as she was.

Charlie had asked to see her and now he stood in front of her, twisting his cap in his hand. 'She's taking it well. I could give it to her, Miss,' he said. Eleanor smiled at him. It was easier to be patient with him now she'd had some sleep. 'Take a few ready bottles and...'

'Put it out of your head,' Eleanor said sharply. She might have known she shouldn't encourage him. 'You're in no state to look after a premature baby.' He looked hurt. Perhaps he didn't realize she would have said the same to any man. 'If you come back in a week or two we can discuss her future.'

'A week or two!' Charlie exclaimed.

'You can visit her every day, if you like,' she said, striving to keep some semblance of patience in her voice. 'I know this is a very difficult time for you, but try to think it out.' She glanced at the baby. 'For May's sake.'

In answer, Charlie shut the door leading to the receiving

146

room. Eleanor started. He could hurt her. It would be so easy…

But all he said was, 'I can't leave her.' He came towards Eleanor, and she had to steel herself not to flinch, even though she no longer thought he meant to harm her. 'I want to. I want to just walk away and never set eyes on her again. You don't know how much I just want to walk away.' The words tumbled out of him, as if he had probably been desperate for someone to talk to.

Probably, in all his life, Clare had been the only one who ever really listened to him, Eleanor thought. And then she wondered, whether, if that had been the case for her father, he would have had the strength to keep her.

'A motherless child is a terrible responsibility,' she said softly.

Charlie came closer. He leaned on the back of a nearby chair. 'Every minute I stop here, me waiting for her, hanging around…' he stopped, as if he couldn't put his feelings into words.

Eleanor supposed it would be hard enough for an educated person. 'Then leave her here,' she said. 'Go home, get back to work. When she's stronger…'

Charlie stood up, almost knocking over the chair in his anger. 'I haven't got a home,' he said, angrily, 'or a job.' Eleanor stared at him. She should have known, she supposed, but he seemed so sure he could look after the baby that she had wanted to believe he could do it. Then he added, 'The police are after me.' Eleanor's eyes widened in shock and he gave her a look that clearly said she could make what she liked of it. 'So I've got to get away,' he said. 'But I've got to take her with me.'

Eleanor couldn't think of anything to say, so after a moment she said the obvious thing. 'What have you done?'

'Thieving, Miss.'

She could see how that would be: how no-one would give an African a job, how he would learn to live in the interstices of society, doing odd jobs here, a bit of pickpocketing there. But to understand was not to condone. 'I could just walk onto the street and call a policeman,' she said.

'You care more about the child than you do about the law,' Charlie said.

There was something almost insolent in his tone, as if he felt he knew her so well he could say what he liked. 'You think I'm a soft touch,' Eleanor said, thinking to herself that he wasn't the only one: as far as she knew all of them – her father, Doctor Marsham, Nurse Carr and Daniel Bentley – thought the same. 'I'm not,' she said firmly.

'I'm all she's got,' Charlie said. The defiance had gone from his eyes now, and despair had replaced it. 'I'll look after her.'

He was begging her. She knew that, but she didn't have anything to give him. 'Charlie, give yourself up,' she said and saw betrayal in his eyes. 'Once you've served your sentence, you can reclaim her.'

He looked away, and Eleanor realized he was striving to keep his temper. 'It will be too late by then,' he said. He looked at her. 'I know what it's like,' he went on. 'One black face in the workhouse?' He was right. Eleanor knew it, deep in her soul. Yet she shook her head as he went on, 'She'll end up like me, or on the streets…'

'I'm sorry,' Eleanor said. 'My first duty is to the child, no matter how much you love her.' At least in the workhouse she would be fed and kept warm and clothed. But Charlie let out a sigh and with it all the fight went out of him. He rubbed his eyes with his hands. He was close to breaking down, that much was plain. 'How long is it since you last slept?' He shrugged. 'Or ate?'

'Before Clare died,' he muttered.

'I'll tell Nurse Carr to get you some tea and bread,' Eleanor said. She got up and turned May round, ready to be burped. 'And Mr Bentley will find you a mattress.' Charlie stared at her, obviously assessing her intentions. 'Don't worry,' she said. 'They won't give you away – we're used to all sorts.'

She rubbed May gently on the back, without letting her gaze waver from Charlie. Eventually, he nodded. Only then did she look down. May was smiling – a windy baby smile, without any meaning behind it, but a smile nevertheless.

'Go on,' she said gently, and Charlie did.

***

Father came to visit late that evening. May and Charlie were both sleeping – May in her makeshift crib, Charlie on a pallet in the attic, having first wolfed down bread and cheese and some stew Nurse Carr had produced for him.

'Well,' Nurse Carr said when she saw Eleanor watching her with a quizzical expression. 'Can't let him starve to death, can I? And he needs hot food to keep out the cold.'

Eleanor thought of that as she did her ward round. Gently, she splinted a lad's leg. It was a clean break without complications. It should heal well enough. Next to her, her father took a microscope from its cherrywood box. The brass gleamed softly in the gaslight. He put it down next to an ether mask and a stethoscope that he was also giving the infirmary.

Eleanor glanced up at him. 'These are pristine,' she

exclaimed. The ether mask looked as if it had never been used. Mr Marsham would be pleased, she thought, turning back to the patient.

There was a bit of a noise from the receiving room as several new patients arrived together. At least one of them had a nasty cough.

'And there are these,' Father said. He proffered Eleanor a box. A set of scalpels nestled in velvet-lined niches. She gasped and patted his arm, knowing what the gesture must be costing him. He smiled. 'Are you always this busy?'

Eleanor grinned ruefully. 'We're usually half-way through the casualties by now.' She tied off the splint.

'When does Marsham get back?' At least he didn't seem angry any more.

'When his father's…' A clatter of boots on floorboards drowned out her words. She looked up, startled. Lady Peters advanced towards her. Behind her were two policemen.

'Oh no,' Eleanor muttered before she could stop herself. She covered her confusion by checking the splint again.

'This is Miss Bramwell, Sergeant,' Lady Peters said. She was resplendent in purple silk and a hat with feathers and a bow. 'I'm sure she knows nothing.'

'Lady Peters, if I might just finish this,' Eleanor said. Anything to buy time.

It didn't work. 'I believe you're looking after a black child, Miss?' the Sergeant said. He had his helmet under his arm, and the badge and his silver buttons winked in the light. 'Fathered by Charlie Carter?'

Eleanor managed to look properly affronted. It wasn't the sort of thing any proper lady would expect to hear. 'I couldn't say who fathered her,' she said, while panic-stricken thoughts tumbled through her mind. If they spot the ladder going up to the attic, they'll look. They will. But Daniel hobbled off on some errand and Nurse Carr found something urgent to do with the enema trolley she had been taking out to the kitchen. If they'd thought of it, they might do something. Only the window looking into the receiving room was directly behind Eleanor. The Sergeant could surely see it from where he was. So if Daniel moved it, he'd just draw attention to it, wouldn't he? And Father knew she was lying. He surely wouldn't say anything with the police there, but...

'He's a thief!' Lady Peters exclaimed. 'A burglar and a footpad and...and...a thief!' she finished, clearly having run out of synonyms.

'Terrorized the area, Miss,' the Sergeant said. Eleanor couldn't quite match that to the man who had wept for his dead wife. Oh, she could see how he might thieve a little, pick a few pockets – but she could also see how every crime would become attached to his name. 'Black Jack,' the Sergeant went on. 'My constable nearly had him, but he's as slippery as...'

'They heard his wife worked for me and they came to the house.' Lady Peters sounded properly scandalized. Eleanor knew what was going through her mind: people will talk. Lady Peters, who loved to gossip – though, Eleanor reminded herself, never maliciously – hated to be the butt of other people's conversation.

'Didn't know she was dead,' the Sergeant went on. 'We reckon he might just come looking for the child.'

Neither Daniel nor Nurse Carr had reappeared. Perhaps they've done it, Eleanor thought. The Sergeant didn't seem to have noticed anything amiss. She forced herself at least to appear calm.

'He could already be here,' Lady Peters said. 'Hiding,' she added, with relish.

It took all Eleanor's willpower not to react. How typical of Lady Peters, she thought – she always does have to get right into the spirit of things.

'Possible, Milady,' the Sergeant said. 'But not likely.'

Good, Eleanor thought. Then off you go.

Lady Peters said, 'Sergeant!' Don't say it, Eleanor thought. Just don't. But Lady Peters went on, 'I'd be very grateful if you'd make absolutely certain. There are sick people here, and if he's dangerous…'

'As the man's black, I think we would have noticed him,' Eleanor cut in, trying to keep her voice light. She stood up.

'No harm in checking, Sergeant,' Father said. Eleanor didn't look at him. She didn't dare. It was clear now that he knew.

'Upstairs, Constable,' the Sergeant said. The man went off to check Daniel's room.

'This way, Sergeant,' Lady Peters said. She led him to the far end of the ward, where May's crib was concealed behind a screen.

'Hello little Black Jack,' the Sergeant said.

Eleanor started. 'Why so tense, Eleanor?' her father asked.

'It's a girl,' came Nurse Carr's prim voice. She was clearly offended. 'May.'

'Good Christian name,' the Sergeant said. 'Wasted on a heathen.'

Eleanor tried not to listen. She needed all her wits to deal with Father. 'I can't believe he's as wicked as they say,' she said weakly.

The Constable came back. 'Only an empty room up there,' he said.

'Right,' said the Sergeant. 'Carry on down here, Constable.'

The man went out into the receiving area. Eleanor glanced through the window. Daniel was slowly mopping the floor. The ladder was nowhere in sight.

'It's not our problem, Eleanor,' Father said. 'Up to the courts.' Eleanor stared at him desperately, knowing there was no time to convince him.

In the silence, Daniel's voice could clearly be heard. 'Rubbish in the alley? Reckon he could be hiding in that?'

Eleanor turned. Daniel and the Constable were standing right under the trapdoor to the attic.

'No, we tried,' the Constable said. Daniel was still mopping, moving slowly down the room away from the trapdoor. 'You ever seen this darkie?' the Constable asked.

'Nah,' Daniel said. 'Don't get 'em in here.'

Father turned on Eleanor. 'We've all seen him!' he hissed. 'What's going on?'

'Nothing!' Eleanor protested, but she couldn't help glancing upwards.

So did Father. She saw him spot the trapdoor, and his expression change from bewilderment to outrage. 'Good God, he's here again,' he said. Eleanor glanced round, terrified someone would hear. 'You've got him, haven't you?' Father demanded.

'He's absolutely exhausted, Father,' Eleanor pleaded in an

undertone. 'He couldn't hurt a fly.'

Her father let out a long, exasperated sigh. 'Sergeant,' he said walking off, 'I think I heard a noise.' For one moment of desperate hope, Eleanor thought perhaps he meant to send them chasing off into the alley. But he went on, 'Yes! In the attic.'

He went into the receiving area. Eleanor could only follow him with the Sergeant close behind. He shouted for the ladder to be brought out. Daniel went for it, hobbling effortfully. Just as they got the ladder in place, Nurse Carr brought the trolley back in.

Lady Peters stared at her as if she'd lost her wits.

'Can't stop work for this nonsense,' the Nurse said shortly.

The Sergeant held the ladder and the Constable went up it, while Daniel stood gawping up at him like an urchin at a stiltwalker. The Constable disappeared into the black maw of the attic. For a moment it seemed to Eleanor that everyone in the room held their breath.

'He's gone!' he shouted. He came down a rung. 'Window's open, Sir. He's had it away on his toes.' He jumped the last couple of rungs.

Eleanor let out her pent-up breath in a slow sigh. He must have seen the policemen and heard their voices through the trapdoor. Good for him, she thought, I'm glad he has escaped.

The Sergeant turned to run for the door, but somehow Daniel managed to be in exactly the wrong place and he couldn't get past.

'Here, I'm crippled, you know,' Daniel said as the Sergeant shoved him roughly aside.

Nurse Carr tut-tutted from where she was working at the trolley. The Sergeant raced past her just as she decided to take the trolley back into the ward. She swung it out, and it caught him in the midriff. He gasped. His hand caught in the enema bowl, and it went flying – and so did its contents, all over the Sergeant's clean uniform.

'Look what you've done!' she said, waving a hand at the few drops that had gone on the floor instead of the Sergeant.

He glared at her but apparently thought better of saying anything. 'Get after him,' he yelled to the Constable.

They dashed out, putting their helmets on as they ran.

Eleanor followed them for a few steps. There was nothing more she could do. As long as they couldn't prove the infirmary staff had known he was there, they were safe.

'What on earth did you think you were doing?' Father demanded, clearly at the end of his patience. 'The man's a common criminal.'

'I was thinking of the child,' Eleanor said, hoping to calm him down. He made an impatient noise and started to walk towards the door. 'And of Charlie,' Eleanor admitted. 'He wants her so much,' she added. Father did not soften. 'What if someone had wrenched me away from you?' she demanded.

He looked at her, clearly hurt; but for that moment she didn't care. She only knew she couldn't leave Charlie to the police. She ran to the door and stood in the streets, peering this way and that through the freezing mist. She could just make out the Constable, running off down the road to her right.

A whistle pierced the night, but it was quite some distance away. A movement in her peripheral vision caught Eleanor's attention. She looked to her left just in time to see Charlie make off down the road at top speed. She turned to go, but just as she got to the door the clatter of cantering horse's hooves made her stop.

She looked round. Charlie came pelting back down the road with a mounted policeman after him, baton raised. As she watched, the baton crashed down on Charlie's shoulders. He slammed into the cobbles.

Eleanor's hand went to her mouth as she stifled a gasp. The policeman dismounted and approached him warily, baton out. Charlie raised his head to watch. At least he's all right, Eleanor thought. The policeman bent down and grabbed Charlie's shoulder. For a moment, Eleanor thought Charlie had given up. Then he surged up and knocked the policeman back. The man's helmet came off and bounced away into the darkness. Charlie slammed him down and pounded his head against the stones.

'Charlie!' Eleanor cried out. The policeman's head slammed into the stones again. 'Charlie.' Once more. At last Charlie looked at her. He got up slowly and stared around wildly. Then he ran off into the night.

In the infirmary, May began to wail.

Chapter 14

There was an argument the next day. Eleanor had known there would be.

'Your drawing room morals don't apply in the Thrift,' she said to Lady Peters, who was standing with her back to the window of the Bramwells' own drawing room.

Lady Peters chopped the air with her hand. 'We must not treat criminals or their families.' She glanced at Eleanor's father for support, but he said nothing.

'That's half the East End ruled out,' Eleanor said. She was flushed. She could feel the heat in her cheeks but she was not going to back down. 'You really mustn't make sweeping rules about whom I may and may not treat.'

'And you mustn't put the infirmary on the wrong side of the law,' Lady Peters snapped back. She drew in a deep breath, causing the copious lace on her bodice to rise and fall.

'I felt I had little choice.' Eleanor rapped out the words. Lady Peters scowled at her. 'If you'd seen Charlie with his baby,' Eleanor said more gently.

'I would have steeled my heart,' said Lady Peters, who was known for many things but not the hardness of her nature.

'Easier said than done,' Father said.

Eleanor looked at him in surprise.

So did Lady Peters. 'Oh,' she said derisively, 'you approve of your daughter harbouring a fugitive?'

'I disapprove of the whole damned Thrift,' he said tartly. He looked from one to the other, like a judge about to deliver a sentence. He turned to Eleanor. 'Now, if you keep breaking the law, they'll shut you down.' Lady Peters smiled triumphantly, but before she could say anything, he turned to her and added, 'And if you want to admit only saints, you shouldn't have opened in the first place.' He sighed. 'Well, the problem's solved now – he abandoned the child and saved his own hide, as we all thought he would.' I didn't, Eleanor thought. Not once I'd seen him with her. I only wish he hadn't beaten that policeman half to death. Father stared at her. 'Well, am I wrong?' She didn't answer, and after a moment he turned to Lady Peters. 'Sherry, my lady?'

'Yes, thank you, Robert,' Lady Peters said. Father went over to the sideboard. The tension between the two women was almost palpable. Lady Peters broke the silence. 'I told Clare's family that mother and child both died,' she said. Eleanor wished that she could be so certain but she said nothing. Things were bad enough between them already. 'I've also found a place for May in the workhouse,' Lady Peters said. She went to join Father. 'As soon as she's well enough we'll send her,' she said as she passed Eleanor.

There was no arguing with her. Eleanor didn't try.

***

Two days later, Eleanor and Daniel followed a grim-faced woman through grimmer corridors. Thin sunlight filtered through the windows set high in the walls, but it hardly seemed to relieve the gloom. Eleanor carried May. Daniel had a pile of clothes and linen for her. It was the best start they could give her.

The woman opened a heavy door and immediately they were assaulted by the wail of several babies crying like lost souls. There was more light inside the room, but that was the only cheer it provided. Two beds were set against the wall and on each there were four babies, wrapped so tightly it was a wonder they could breathe, never mind wave their arms or legs.

Opposite them, a child of four at most sat on a low stool. She was dressed in a thin shift. When they came in, she was playing with a bit of rag, holding it up and folding and refolding it. As soon as she saw it she dropped it and looked at them guiltily.

Daniel looked round the room. 'They look well fed, anyway,' he said, though how he could tell under the swaddling Eleanor didn't know. Then she understood – he and Nurse Carr had both grown fond of the little mite. They didn't want to lose her any more than Eleanor did, especially not to a place like this. Daniel pointed awkwardly to the toddler. She made a fist of her hand and gnawed at it, patently terrified of them. 'That one'll be keeping an eye on them,' Daniel said. 'Not a kid for long in a place like this.' He turned to Eleanor. 'Workhouse brat, me, Doctor.' She stared at him, appalled. She had had no idea. He turned back and said to the infants on the bed, 'This is as good as it's ever going to get, babbies. Make the most of it.'

The worst of it was, he was right. Eleanor could feel it deep inside – the despair seeping in. She looked at May, who was sleeping peacefully: golden skin and brown hair, so different from the workhouse pallor. However bad it was for the babies on the bed, it would be worse for her. Daniel turned back to her. 'Leave her on the bed, shall we?' He reached for her.

Eleanor jerked her away. 'No,' she said. He looked shocked and she added more quietly, 'No, Mr Bentley, I don't think so.'

Daniel smiled at her. They walked quickly away, and then out of the workhouse and into the sunshine. With every step she took away from it, Eleanor's heart rose.

***

Eleanor's eyes flicked open. She lay in the warmth of her bed, momentarily confused. She had been dreaming. Something about her mother. It was gone.

There was a noise from downstairs. Surely not, she thought. Perhaps it was the wind in the trees, rattling the branches against the windows. But it came again and she realized she had heard it before.

There was no point in staying where she was. She got out of bed and grabbed her dressing gown, then lit a lamp. By its tiny circle of light, she slipped out of her room, taking great care to be silent.

When she was half-way down the stairs, she saw Father emerging from the understairs cupboard. He was carrying his old service rifle.

'Stay there,' he hissed at her. He was loading shells into the gun.

'I'll fetch the groom,' she whispered back.

'No. You stay there.' He clicked the rifle shut and snapped the safety catch off.

Without waiting for an answer, he went over to the drawing room doors. He paused for a moment, listening. Then he barged both doors open and thrust the gun up in front of him.

'Stand still or I'll shoot,' he commanded. 'Move slowly into the middle of the room.'

Eleanor went down to join him, now that she was certain he was in control of the situation. 'Charlie!' she exclaimed.

He stood in the glare of her oil lamp, holding up his empty hands. He blinked against the light. 'I tried throwing stones up at the windows, but I didn't know which one,' he said.

'I heard something,' Eleanor said. 'But I thought it was the wind.'

'What the hell are you doing here?' demanded Father. The rifle hadn't wavered from its aim.

'Not robbing us, Father,' Eleanor said, trying to calm him. 'Trying to wake us.' She set the lamp down on the table. 'Put the gun away.'

He didn't, but Charlie slowly lowered his hands.

'How's May?' he asked.

'Well,' Eleanor said, moving round as she spoke until she was between the two men. 'Quite well.' She couldn't repress her smile. 'She's getting fat.'

'There are police all around the place,' Charlie said. 'I tried to get back in, but no chance.'

'Eleanor,' Father said. 'I think you should fetch the groom.'

Charlie licked his lips.

'He's not doing us any harm,' protested Eleanor.

'He's a wanted man.'

'Can she take milk now?' Charlie asked as if Eleanor's father had never spoken. 'Cow's milk?'

'No,' Eleanor said. Honesty compelled her to add, 'We haven't tried.'

'I've found a boat willing to take us to France,' Charlie said. 'Leaves tomorrow, midnight.' He glanced at Father. 'Land in the north, make our way to Marseille. More of my kind there.'

'You'll never get past the police,' Eleanor cut in.

'Yes,' Charlie admitted. 'But you will. Please, Miss,' he begged, 'will you bring the baby out to me?' Eleanor licked her lips. 'You have to,' he urged.

'How will you manage?' she asked to give herself time to think.

'Eleanor, it's a child not a doll,' Father said, clearly furious. He turned to Charlie. 'You leave her hungry for a few hours and she'll starve before you know it.'

'I won't let her,' Charlie said. It was obvious he meant it, Eleanor decided, but whether he understood what he was trying to do was another thing entirely. 'I don't know what we'll do when we are there, but I know what kind of life she'll lead here. I don't want her on the streets in a few years.' His fists clenched. 'I want something better.'

It was what all parents wanted wasn't it? Eleanor thought. The best for their children; or if not the best, then better than what they themselves had had. You couldn't fault the man's desire, only his ability to provide it.

Father, however, was not swayed. 'And she will get it, will she', he rapped out, 'from a notorious villain on the run from the hangman?'

'What are they hanging me for?' Charlie whispered, clearly shocked.

'Your fight with the Constable,' Eleanor said gently. The man had made a good recovery but that wouldn't count

162

with any judge.

Charlie breathed hard, once. His lips skinned back from his teeth. Then he got control. 'Please,' he said, 'bring me my daughter.'

'I don't know,' Eleanor said. She was too tired to weigh one interest against the other – the child's against the man's; or even, really, to know any more what the child's interests were.

'I'll be at Battery Quay, tomorrow at eleven,' Charlie said. There was a hardness about him, born, Eleanor was quite certain, of absolute despair. 'If you are not there, I won't give up. Wherever you send her, I'll find her.' He looked from Eleanor to her father. 'Somehow.'

'Then you'll be arrested for kidnapping,' Father pointed out.

'And they'll try me for that after they've hanged me, will they?' Charlie came back, quick as could be. 'Put your gun down, before you blow your daughter's head off.'

There was something sullen in his tone that let Eleanor see for the first time what in his character had led him into bad ways. Yet she couldn't, truly, believe he was wholly bad; given a better start, she thought, who knows what he might have done with that sharp wit.

He went to the window but before he went through it, he said, 'Battery Quay. Eleven.' Then he was gone.

Somewhere, a dog began to bark. Eleanor shut the window against the noise and the cold night air.

'So the child's in the workhouse, is she?' Father said when she turned round.

Eleanor shook her head ruefully. 'I couldn't.' She smiled. Father scowled back at her.

Eleanor didn't try to raise the subject the next morning until breakfast was nearly over and Father was on his third cup of coffee.

'He's a liar and a thief,' he declared.

'But he doesn't deserve to be hanged,' Eleanor said. 'And whatever else he may be, he wants to be a good father.'

Her father was having none of it. 'Do not try to manipulate my feelings again,' he said. 'If you want to do something silly with this child, then do so.' He popped a last piece of toast into his mouth. 'But don't take me along with you.'

'You wouldn't try to stop me?'

'No,' Father said slowly. 'When your mother died, your grandparents wanted you,' he went on, and Eleanor realized she didn't have to manipulate his feelings this time: he was doing a fine job by himself. 'Your Aunt Alice was convinced she should have you. No-one believed a widower could bring up a child on his own. Sometimes, after a long day when you'd been particularly tiresome and charming and difficult, I thought they were right.'

Eleanor grinned, realizing that they were no longer fighting. 'And now?' she asked.

'Now I know they were right.' He smiled at her fondly. Eleanor chuckled. 'I never thought of parting with you,' he said. 'Your birth made your life so precious – so near to death, yet full of life…' He paused, clearly remembering that night, that moment in which he'd known he was tied to her. 'Well, I saw that look in Charlie's eyes that first night, when he held May.' He shook his head, clearly bewildered by the decision he was reaching. 'He couldn't have faked that. Perhaps he deserves a chance. Or May does.'

He got up and walked round behind Eleanor. He put his hands on her shoulders. She looked up at him. 'And what if she dies on the voyage?' She was looking for easy reassurance. She didn't get it.

'Playing with lives, Eleanor. It's never an easy game.' He walked away. 'It's never a game.'

***

There was a large and rather battered perambulator in the treatment room of the Thrift. Eleanor stared at it.

Daniel limped over. 'Good, eh, Doctor?' he said, grinning. 'Takes two nippers and a sack of coal no trouble. You can borrow it till our next.' He leaned on it to show off the suspension. 'Bringing the cot tomorrow,' he said proudly.

'May won't be here for ever, Mr Bentley,' Eleanor said. It had never occurred to her that others might have become as attached to May as she had.

'No, but she'll be here a while, won't she?' Daniel protested. 'People's funny about darkies, even a nice little creature like her.' Nurse Carr came over and laid May gently in the perambulator.

'Has Lady Peters seen May recently?' Eleanor asked carefully.

'No, Miss,' replied Nurse Carr. She smiled meaningfully. 'The child's always fast asleep when she comes.'

'In the linen closet,' Daniel added.

'Just as well,' Eleanor said, relieved. She wanted no more arguments. 'Until we find her a nice home.'

'Nice homes won't be queuing up for her, Miss,' Nurse Carr said. 'How you'll make sure she's not ill treated I don't know.'

'No point worrying about it, is there though?' Daniel said. 'I mean, she's going to have a rough enough life whatever we do, poor little heathen.'

Eleanor made her decision in that moment: better, she decided, to have a rough life with a loving father than a rough life with no-one who cared.

***

Eleanor's boots clattered on the cobbles. They were slick with seawater and she was scared she might slip with the baby in her arms. She peered into the darkness. Boxes and bales and coils of rope were piled up, dark on dark, on the quayside, and a barrow with a broken wheel lay on its side. Anyone could be hiding there. But it was the sounds that made the night truly terrifying: the creak of a ship's rigging competed with the lapping of the waves against the wharf. Suddenly, she heard shouts. A fight, somewhere up ahead.

'Charlie,' she whispered querulously.

Someone coughed. She whirled round. A man staggered out of the shadows, clutching his scarf to his throat. He reeled past her.

She walked on, trying to look everywhere at once. Somewhere, someone was whistling. She moved in that direction, wondering what she would do if she couldn't find him. Send May to the workhouse after all, she supposed.

'Charlie?' she called again.

A movement caught her eye. She twisted round. Nothing.

'Don't drop the baby, Miss,' said Charlie's voice from behind her. She turned, swallowing hard, trying anything to disguise her fear, now that it was receding. 'You have got her?' he asked, suddenly anxious.

Eleanor brought out May from under her cloak. She was wrapped in blankets inside a basket. 'And two feeds,' Eleanor said. She would have liked to make it more, but they would only have spoiled, even in this weather; and two would see May safe on dry land, all being well. 'She should be all right till mid-day tomorrow.' She pulled out the bag Nurse Carr had prepared. 'Some clothes,' she explained.

'Thanks,' Charlie said. He hooked the bag of clothes over his shoulder. 'Give her here,' he said.

Eleanor looked at the baby. She realized she was almost in tears. 'If there were any other way…' she said and realized that if she could have found a way to raise the child herself she would have.

'There isn't,' Charlie pointed out.

Eleanor forced calmness on herself. Think of the practicalities, she decided. That always worked. 'You must keep her dry and clean,' she said. 'She'll be subject to fevers for some months.' She realized she was hoping to put him off the whole mad plan, even now.

'I'll do my best,' Charlie said. 'She must take her chance with me, Miss. It's not what I want, but it's the best on offer.' Eleanor nodded. It was only what she had already worked out herself. Yet she still couldn't do it. 'Miss?' he said.

Finally, Eleanor held out the basket. Charlie reached out and scooped up his baby, leaving the basket behind. Eleanor found she was watching him through tear-blurred eyes. She fumbled in her bag. 'Here's some money,' she said, unable to bring herself to look at them any more. She found the purse she wanted. 'My father had some French francs…'

She looked up. Charlie had already gone.

167

***

Lady Peters came to visit the next day. She sat taking coffee with them, while the police Sergeant – brought by her for the purpose – explained that nothing had been seen of Charlie Carter for days, and they could, therefore, sleep easy in their beds.

Father saw him to the door. Eleanor perched on the edge of her seat, trying not to appear terribly interested in the conversation going on in the hall. She wished Kate would hurry up with the coffee – holding a cup and saucer would give her something to do with her hands.

'Well, I'm sure you're right, Sergeant,' Father said heartily. 'He'll be making for Liverpool, Bristol – somewhere big enough for him to start all over again.'

'Robbing and creating mayhem,' the Sergeant said, sourly.

'Indeed,' Father answered. There was the sound of the door opening. 'Well, thank you so much for keeping us informed. Good day, Sergeant.'

The door clicked shut. Eleanor restrained a sigh.

Father came back in. He smiled at Lady Peters. 'Of course,' he mused, 'he could still be here somewhere – hiding in the tenements.'

'He could be hop picking in Kent,' Lady Peters said. She was wearing maroon velvet today. 'They do that, you know.'

Kate brought over the tray. 'Cook says he's probably hopped it to France,' she said. Eleanor tried to glare at her, without actually letting Lady Peters see what she was doing. If her expression were anything like the one Father was currently wearing, she was making a bad job of it. 'Sorry, Sir,' Kate said. She stared up at Father miserably.

'Well, Kate, cook could possibly be right,' Father said after a moment.

'It's very unlikely though,' added Eleanor quickly. 'Thank you Kate,' she added as a dismissal.

Kate hurried off.

If Lady Peters noticed anything amiss, she gave no sign of it. Probably thinks we have a problem with impertinent servants who speak out of turn, Eleanor decided; and with luck her sense of good manners would stop her mentioning it.

Perhaps Eleanor was right. In any event, Lady Peters changed the subject herself. 'I must find out how the child is getting on in the workhouse,' she said, and chinked her cup down on her saucer.

'I don't think you should do that,' Eleanor said far too quickly. She glanced at Father but he gave her no help. 'You made a professional decision, and professionals shouldn't get involved.'

Lady Peters looked startled. Eleanor supposed that, coming from her, it must seem a little out of character.

'Besides,' Father put in smoothly, 'you have enough patients at present in the Thrift without worrying about past ones.'

Lady Peters smiled at Eleanor. 'Hark at him,' she said. 'I thought he was quite taken with little May, didn't you?'

Eleanor smiled too, as flirtatious as ever Lady Peters could wish. 'My father? Interested in motherless babes?' she asked coquettishly. 'According to him, they're nothing but trouble.' She leaned a little closer to Lady Peters. 'For years and years.'

'Decades,' Father said.

Chapter 15

'And ten shillings for Mr Bentley,' Lady Peters said. Eleanor looked up just in time to see her slam the ledger shut. 'Do try to get some sort of signature this time,' she said. She stood up and brought the ledger and the pen, in its inkwell, over to Eleanor's desk.

She seemed a little tired, Eleanor thought; but perhaps it was just a trick of the light, or the fact that today, for the first time since Eleanor had known her, she was wearing a pale-coloured dress, since she had been in mourning for her husband a decently long time.

Eleanor smiled at her. 'He can make a mark,' she said, 'but he can't write.'

A scream drowned out her last few words. Through the open door she saw a man being stretchered into the receiving room. Eleanor ignored it: Doctor Marsham was on duty.

Lady Peters walked away from Eleanor's desk. 'Then he must learn,' she said. 'We can't have a staff of uncultured labourers.'

'Ten shillings a week won't get us a university professor,' Eleanor said. She had come to love Lady Peters dearly, but sometimes her ideas were simply impracticable.

Daniel's voice came to them from the receiving room, where he was trying to clear out all but the most urgent cases:

it seemed harsh, but otherwise none of the staff would ever have seen their homes. 'When I say out,' he bellowed, 'I mean out. Now move.'

Eleanor glanced over to Lady Peters, who was holding up a small picture to the light. It seemed to her that he was of considerably more use to them than a university professor would have been.

Lady Peters seemed to have caught her thought, for she said, 'No, Mr Bentley's perfectly acceptable.' She sighed. 'It's just that there's room for improvement,' she walked back to Eleanor's desk and held up the picture to the wall, 'as in most things round here.' She took down the picture again. There really wasn't room for it, a fact for which Eleanor gave due thanks. It was almost grotesque in its sentimentality: a girl in flounces and furbelows leaning on a wet-eyed Saint Bernard dog. 'Mrs Protheroe donated it,' Lady Peters explained. 'Cheerful little thing, isn't it?' It was clear from her smile that she was going to find somewhere to put it.

Eleanor smiled back weakly.

'Right,' Daniel bellowed from the receiving room. 'Anybody else not bleeding or dying, get off home and come back tomorrow.'

Lady Peters went to stand just inside the receiving room. 'We really should shut the doors earlier,' she said, as if it were the most obvious thing in the world. 'I'm sure there aren't queues at the East London at this time of night.'

Eleanor took the pile of swabs to the cupboard in the receiving room. As she went past Lady Peters, she said, 'We're not the East London, and you'd hate it if we were.' She kept her voice light, but Lady Peters had been finding things to niggle

171

over for days – weeks, even – and she was beginning to lose patience.

'Why?' Lady Peters demanded. 'The bigger we are, the more people we can help. Why be content with six beds, when we could have sixteen? Or sixty,' she said, getting excited.

'This isn't a sewing circle,' Eleanor reproved her. 'We can't just pack everything away tidily at teatime.' Lady Peters looked away, obviously miffed. 'And if we had six hundred beds, there'd still be people waiting at the end of the day.'

Lady Peters turned back to her. There was a glint in her eye that made Eleanor wish she hadn't spoken. 'Six hundred…' she mused. 'That really would be a monument to my husband's memory.' She walked off into the receiving room, obviously much taken with the idea.

Good, thought Eleanor. It was a completely impossible notion, but it might just take her mind off the horrid picture. Then she realized that Lady Peters was still carrying it and trying it out in various positions around the room.

Eleanor sighed and went into the ward to find out about the young man who had been brought in earlier.

Doctor Marsham came over to meet her. 'Name's Wilf Baker,' he said. 'Broken neck by the look of it, but there's a deal of bruising, so I can't be sure. He got caught in a cave-in working on the underground railway.'

'Any other fractures?'

'None obvious, but he's no feeling.'

'We'll just have to wait for the bruising to go,' Eleanor said and waited for Doctor Marsham's inevitable objections.

'It could take days,' he said. 'We have people needing operations.'

Eleanor knew he had a point but she was also quite sure that at home he would be propped up in a chair and left in a corner to turn into a human vegetable. It was an impossible decision, though no harder than others she faced every day.

Lady Peters interrupted her thoughts. 'Then we could put him in an...' she hesitated, 'X-radiography machine.' She pronounced the unusual words carefully.

'I beg your pardon, Lady Peters?' Doctor Marsham said, as he and Eleanor turned to her.

She was holding up the picture to the kitchen wall, but she stopped and let it hang loosely in one hand. 'Look through the flesh into the very bones,' she said, as if that explained everything. 'I learned all about it at dinner,' she said, as they stared at her.

'X-radiography?' Eleanor said, hoping for a better explanation.

'It's a technique to reveal a living skeleton with no surgery,' Doctor Marsham said. 'I've read a paper,' he added.

He had always been determined to keep up with every advance; Eleanor remembered that he had once told her he needed all the edge he could get. She realized somewhat guiltily that she couldn't remember when she had last read a research paper, let alone what it had been about.

'Sir Herbert has one at the East London,' Lady Peters said.

Aha, Eleanor thought, realizing where the older woman had had dinner the night before.

'I'm sure he has,' Doctor Marsham said. 'He loves his new gadgets.' There was just a hint of wistfulness in his tone.

For all the good it does us or that poor lad, Eleanor thought resentfully. 'It's just patients he has no time for,' Eleanor said.

'And female doctors.' Doctor Marsham laughed, and so did she. But she was honest enough to admit to herself that there was an underlying bitterness to her words. Apparently, all her work at the Thrift was not enough to expunge it.

'Well,' Lady Peters said, with uncharacteristic diffidence, 'he's seeing me tomorrow...' Is he now? Eleanor wondered. She hadn't realized he was Lady Peters' physician. 'I could ask him if we may borrow it,' she finished. She went back to trying to place the picture.

'It's a massive contraption,' Doctor Marsham said.

Lady Peters turned. 'All you need is a little imagination,' she said, smiling coquettishly.

'Even the wildest imagination couldn't see Sir Herbert helping us,' Eleanor said. She smiled, to make a joke of it, but part of her was serious: she hated the thought of Lady Peters being embarrassed by a refusal.

'Wait and see, Eleanor,' Lady Peters said, and would say no more.

***

The next afternoon, Lady Peters came into the Thrift resplendent in a pale mauve dress with a collar of ivory lace, and full of excitement.

'Not that I'm one to say "I told you so", Eleanor,' she crowed. 'But I told you so!'

***

The next morning at seven-thirty they wheeled Wilf along the corridor of the East London, towards the operating theatre. Eleanor pushed, while Doctor Marsham pulled the front, so he could talk to Wilf to keep him calm; Lady Peters cleared the way for them.

'After looking at your bones, we'll get your head read,' he said, bending low as he walked, so that the boy could hear him. 'Try and cure you of this football nonsense.'

There was a linen hamper in the way. Eleanor stopped while Lady Peters pushed it away. It must have been heavy, for it seemed to take her a lot of effort to move it.

'I have to be out by Saturday, Doctor,' Wilf protested. 'Clapburn Rovers is in the Cup Final.'

Lady Peters finally managed to push the hamper back, and Eleanor and Doctor Marsham moved the trolley on. As Eleanor went past, she saw that Lady Peters was leaning on the hamper to get her breath back. Sweet old thing, she thought, always determined to do her bit.

'All this sneaking in like this,' Lady Peters said. She sounded out of breath. Eleanor heard her pattering along behind, trying to catch up, and slowed down for her. 'It's not necessary,' she went on, finally catching up. 'Sir Herbert really was most accommodating.'

'I'm sure he was,' Eleanor said crisply. 'Delighted to have me returning cap in hand.'

'But you needn't be here,' Lady Peters pointed out. 'Doctor Marsham and I can manage.'

Eleanor scowled. That would have been altogether too easy. She had never liked easy solutions. 'Oh, he'd love that,' she said. 'Poor, foolish Miss Bramwell – frightened to show her face.'

Doctor Marsham turned to her. He was, she noticed, dressed in his best coat and bowler hat. 'He never turns up till mid-morning. We won't have to see him.' I can only hope, Eleanor thought. 'Ah, here we are,' Doctor Marsham said. He brought the trolley to a stop outside a pair of double doors Eleanor remembered only too well.

Lady Peters hurried forward. 'Allow me,' she said. She opened the door. Doctor Marsham turned the trolley and led it in. Eleanor followed...

'Oh!' Lady Peters said. 'Quite a stitch!'

...and found herself confronting a roomful of medical students. They were seated in raised tiers around the periphery of the room. Sir Herbert was standing on the floor of the theatre, like an actor taking centre stage.

'Doctor Marsham, Miss Bramwell,' he said with a flourish of his hand, 'good morning to you both.'

There was nothing for it but to allow the attendants to push the trolley into the middle of the room.

'Gentlemen,' he said, turning to the students. 'Here we have a possible broken spine.' He gestured to the trolley. 'This unfortunate fellow was taken to a local...' he paused, and turned as if puzzled. 'What would you call your little charity, Miss Bramwell?'

'It's an infirmary,' Eleanor said stonily. She had known that Sir Herbert's only purpose in helping them was to humiliate her; but she had not expected it to hurt so much.

'Yes, of course it is,' Sir Herbert, in the sort of tone he might have used to agree with a small child who had just told him that a horse was, in fact, a dragon. He turned back to the students. 'A small infirmary,' he said.

'I believe I know the one, Sir,' Caslow said. Eleanor glared at him; she had quite managed to put his noxious personality out of her mind. He turned to the other students: it seemed he had learned how to grandstand from Sir Herbert, along with

176

any medicine he might have managed to pick up. 'I was only saying the other day, "That building would have made an excellent radio X-ray department." ' That won him a scattering of laughter.

'And so it could,' Sir Herbert agreed. 'Where this...' he glanced down at the trolley, as if to check who he was dealing with today: he probably needs to, Eleanor thought – it would be beneath the great Sir Herbert to remember a patient from one moment to the next, 'ah...young man', Sir Herbert went on, 'could have received the treatment he needs in a properly scientific environment.'

'But Wilf has no money, so I doubt if you'd have seen him at all,' Eleanor said tartly. 'Unless you've changed the rules?' she added sweetly.

Sir Herbert was facing the students, so Eleanor couldn't see his face, but his opinion was clear from the way his shoulders tensed.

Caslow leaned forward. 'Isn't there a rule about women doctors in the operating theatre, Sir Herbert?' he asked.

Eleanor bit her lip. Somehow she was certain that she had just walked into a trap: she thought she had learned Sir Herbert's wiles better than that.

'Oh come, come, Mr Caslow,' Sir Herbert protested. 'Let's not be ungracious.'

'I'm just saying, Sir,' Caslow said mildly. 'And she was the one to mention rules...' Now Eleanor was certain: they had arranged this between them.

'Well,' Sir Herbert answered, 'you may be right.' He turned to Eleanor. 'You see, Miss Bramwell, after your dismissal the Board decided no more ladies.' It doesn't matter what I said, she thought. They'd have worked round to it somehow and managed to make it my own fault too. 'So perhaps you'd better wait outside…' Sir Herbert finished. Eleanor glared at him. It was the fake sympathy in his voice that she really couldn't bear. She glanced at Doctor Marsham, though she knew there was nothing he could do. 'Mr Caslow, the door,' Sir Herbert said.

Mr Caslow ran across the theatre to open it. Eleanor swept past him with what dignity she could muster.

Outside, she paced up and down the corridor, up and down. That she was stuck out here while Sir Herbert performed who knew what barbarisms on her patient – her patient – was more than she could bear.

She turned to say as much to Lady Peters, but the older woman looked guilty enough. Tired, too, Eleanor thought, considering the pallor of her skin and the way she was leaning heavily against the wall. If she hadn't interfered, she thought…and dismissed it immediately as unworthy. She couldn't bring herself to speak to her, though.

***

Later, when Nurse Carr had shown her the result of Sir Herbert's treatment – a huge burn on Wilf's chest – Eleanor found it harder to keep silent.

'I don't care how nice he was to you,' she snapped at Lady Peters as she prepared Wilf's dressing. 'He treats his patients like sides of beef.'

Lady Peters walked slowly towards her. 'Sir Herbert is a well-respected physician,' she protested.

'Arrogant and determined to contradict at every turn.' Eleanor was shouting now. She didn't care.

'Please,' Lady Peters said. 'I have a laudanum headache.'

She sat down at the desk. 'I barely slept. Sir Herbert says I need calm and quiet.'

Eleanor glanced at her. She did seem drawn. 'And he'd know, would he?' She couldn't understand how Lady Peters could have gone to him in the first place, but if that was her choice, Eleanor certainly wasn't going to interfere. She slapped a burns dressing on the bandage with a brush. 'After burning a damned great hole in Wilf's chest.'

Doctor Marsham came in. 'Never again,' he said as he closed the door behind him. 'We'll do without cathode rays in the future,' he said pointedly, looking at Lady Peters. He went to the table where Eleanor was working and leaned on it. 'If he didn't have a broken spine before, he's probably got one now.'

Eleanor saw Lady Peters shake her head in pain or irritation, but she couldn't help herself. 'And all we got was a blurred mess which even the engineer couldn't understand.'

'Whether his spine's broken or not, we can't discharge him with that burn,' said Doctor Marsham.

That'll please Nurse Carr, Eleanor thought; she had been adamant that they should give the bruising time to heal before they decided whether or not his case was hopeless. Doctor Marsham had been equally determined that they should discharge him as soon as possible, and the disagreement had created a terrible atmosphere.

'Is that his dressing?' Doctor Marsham asked.

Eleanor only nodded. She was scared that if she spoke she would say something which would offend Lady Peters completely.

Nurse Carr came in, rescuing her. 'How could they do that to him, Doctor?' she asked.

'It wasn't what any of us intended, Nurse,' Doctor Marsham said, bitterly.

It seemed that Wilf was not the only one wounded by the incident.

***

That night, as Eleanor and her father sat together by the fire in the parlour, she told him what had happened.

'Exploration of the body by cathode ray,' father mused. His newspaper crackled against his lap as he moved. 'It's a new science.' He looked at Eleanor as if daring her to contradict him. 'Eventually Sir Herbert will master it.' She raised her eyebrows at him. 'After a fashion,' he added, wryly. He went back to his broadsheet.

Eleanor fiddled with her neckchain. 'The knighthood did wonders for his reputation,' she said, staring into the flames. 'It's a pity it couldn't make him a better surgeon.' She raised her hand and shook it, as if alcohol had made it tremble.

'Oh, he used to be good,' Father said. 'People remember that.' He looked at her speculatively. 'He has some influence. You should learn from Lady Peters – pamper the man's ego and he'll eat out of your hand.'

'Nauseating thought to end the day with,' Eleanor said. She got up and kissed him on the cheek. 'Thank you, Father,' she added drily and left him to his paper.

***

Eleanor walked across the receiving room of the Thrift, carrying a bowlful of antiseptic and some swabs. The outer door swung open and Lady Peters came in.

'Lady Peters,' Eleanor said, 'I thought you were resting today.' She certainly seemed to need it – her colour was somewhat better but there were deep shadows under her eyes.

'I've brought along an old friend to see all the good we're doing,' Lady Peters answered.

She gestured towards the door. Sir Herbert walked in. Eleanor swallowed. How could Lady Peters betray her so? How could she not see that this was betrayal?

'Well, well,' Sir Herbert said, as if he were some favourite but rarely seen uncle. 'Here we are, Miss Bramwell.' He looked around, obviously assessing the Thrift already.

'Sir Herbert,' Eleanor said.

'I had to come', he said leaning too close to her, 'because I was aware the other day of some coolness between us.'

'Were you?' Eleanor said; it was her opinion that his sensitivity might lead him to notice coolness – if he were standing in the arctic.

'I've no objection to you or any other charming young lady being in my operating theatre,' he looked from Eleanor to Lady Peters, who was at least old enough to be his sister, if not his wife. 'But, you know – rules are rules and Caslow is an awkward fellow.' He smiled. 'I wanted to assure you of my good wishes and fellow-feeling.'

'I see,' said Eleanor. There was a silence which it was obvious Lady Peters and Sir Herbert expected her to fill. She did not.

'Sir Herbert is very intrigued by our water supply,' Lady Peters said at last.

There was a sound behind Eleanor. She turned to see Doctor Marsham coming to join them.

'Yes,' Sir Herbert said, as if he had her full attention. 'Three sinks and a sluice, I'm told, for only six beds.' From his tone,

Eleanor thought, one might have thought it was a barbaric condition, not an ample supply.

'Hygiene not just for the patients but for the physicians too, Sir,' Doctor Marsham said.

Sir Herbert laughed as if that were a great joke. 'Do you know, I can hardly persuade any of my students to touch water – unless it's in whisky.' He glanced at Lady Peters, who smiled appreciatively.

'We have the advantage of being sober most of the time,' Eleanor said. She smiled, though she didn't intend it as a joke. It wasn't taken as such.

'Well now,' Lady Peters said brightly, clearly determined to rescue the situation. 'Who's going to show Sir Herbert around? He's bound to ask medical questions.'

'Mr Marsham?' Eleanor said.

'Of course,' he replied, though he was clearly not very happy with the idea. 'Follow me, Sir.'

'Thank you,' Sir Herbert said. As he passed Eleanor, he stopped and squeezed her arm. She endured it silently, but as soon as he turned away, she rubbed at the place as if to scrub away a stain.

Lady Peters pursed her lips. It was clear that she required some sort of explanation.

When the men were out of earshot, Eleanor said, 'I've work to do.' Lady Peters continued to stare at her. 'I'm sorry,' Eleanor snapped. 'I refuse to flirt and gush all over him.' She turned on her heel and strode away to finish the dressing she had started earlier.

She heard Lady Peters following her and glanced up from her work. The other woman had advanced a few steps but was clinging to the back of one of the benches. She had her gloved hand to her mouth, but when she saw Eleanor looking at her she took it away. 'If it helps this infirmary,' she said, 'I would happily flirt with the devil himself.' She swallowed hard. 'But I really must have a cup of tea before I gush any more!' She let go of the bench and put her hand to her stomach for a moment. Then she went off towards the kitchen.

Eleanor continued to work for a moment. Then she dropped the swab into the dirty tray and went after Lady Peters. She hated there to be unpleasantness between them; but she hated having Sir Herbert in her infirmary even more.

She found Lady Peters searching for the tea-caddy.

'There are still as many sick people needing us now as when we opened,' Lady Peters said. She banged a cupboard shut.

What did she expect? Eleanor wondered. That we, alone, would eradicate consumption from the East End, improve working conditions so that accidents are eliminated, and find a cure for birth defects, all in our first year? Her great fear was that Lady Peters might just come to believe it was possible – with the help of Sir Herbert and the backing of the East London. 'And there always will be,' she said. 'Sir Herbert couldn't do anything about that – he's more likely to bar people from the place than encourage them.'

'Don't be so silly,' Lady Peters said. She made an impatient chopping gesture with her hand, as if to cut off the conversation. 'Can't the night staff do all this washing?' she said, looking round at the piles of dirty sheet and towels.

'They do all they can,' Eleanor said. She didn't intend to be sidetracked, no matter how uncomfortable it made Lady

Peters. 'His reputation and his pride mean more to him than anything else.' She couldn't bring herself to say Sir Herbert's name. Lady Peters looked at her sharply. 'Truly,' Eleanor insisted.

Lady Peters washed a cup. 'You have no monopoly on caring,' she said. 'He's already making my life easier. Just mention his name and doors open.' She dried the cup and put it on the bench.

'We're doing very well without him,' Eleanor pointed out.

Lady Peters started to look for the tea again. 'With two overworked doctors and an exhausted administrator?' Lady Peters demanded. She got the teapot out of the bottom cupboard.

'You're exaggerating,' Eleanor said. They all got tired at times. There was really no need for Lady Peters to make all this fuss, like a fractious child up after its bedtime.

'Suppose one of us should fall ill,' Lady Peters said, 'how would this place continue?' She waved the teapot around to emphasize her point. 'I have to make provision for the future, regardless of petty squabbles between professionals.'

So that's it, Eleanor thought. She's jealous that Mr Marsham and I do all the real work here, while she's left to look after the books. She didn't say it though; she knew if she did there might be no repairing the rift it would cause.

She glanced at Lady Peters. The older woman was rubbing her forehead. No doubt she has another laudanum headache, courtesy of Sir Herbert, Eleanor thought.

'I've accepted an invitation to talk with Sir Herbert and his hospital governors on Friday morning,' Lady Peters said. She gripped the edges of the table 'You, me and Mr Marsham.'

'What for?' demanded Eleanor.

Lady Peters crossed in front of her and, with a triumphant little cry, extracted the caddy from under a teatowel. 'To discuss how they and we can work together for the benefit of the sick.' She flipped open the caddy. Light glinted on its empty interior. She sighed. 'I'll have a glass of hot water,' she said. 'It seems to be the only thing we have in plenty here.'

And plenty of dissension, if this goes on, Eleanor thought sourly.

***

They rode in silence to the East London, that Friday morning, in Lady Peters' carriage. The atmosphere was frosty, but no more than it was in the days following Lady Peters' announcement.

***

The boardroom of the East London Hospital might have been designed to intimidate. Eleanor, Doctor Marsham and Lady Peters sat on one side of a table; opposite them, across what seemed like an acre or so of polished mahogany, sat the board members – as hoary a collection of old duffers as you could hope to find, Eleanor thought. But Sir Herbert was chief among them, seated exactly in the middle of them. She reminded herself not to underestimate him. No more walking into his beartraps, she told herself firmly. That was going to be hard to do, however, with Lady Peters at her side, swooning over his every word.

Once they had exchanged pleasantries – or at least such pleasantries as Eleanor was prepared to exchange – Sir Herbert said, 'We can either provide your infirmary with those facilities not yet funded by public donation or we could open our hospital for your use.' It was a generous offer, thought Eleanor; far too generous to be genuine. They weren't going to offer all that without getting something back for it. 'I rather think that the ideal would be a mixture of the two,' Sir Herbert added. He steepled his hands in front of him. Early-morning sunlight gleamed on the gold of his watch and cufflinks, and picked out copper highlights in his ginger hair and beard. He smiled.

The smile on the face of the tiger, Eleanor thought.

'That sounds very interesting,' Lady Peters said.

It sounds like an attempt to swallow us whole, Eleanor thought. She decided there was no point in evading the issue. 'Why, suddenly, after so long on our own with no help from anyone – why are you now so supportive?' she asked. She strove to keep her anger out of her voice, and thought she succeeded.

'Because colleagues should support one another,' Sir Herbert said, in his talking-to-children voice. As you supported me when you had me dismissed for daring to question you? Eleanor wondered. But she did not dare voice the thought. She had promised Lady Peters that she would at least listen to what they had to say, and she intended to keep that promise: it would make her rejection, when she made it, appear all the more reasonable. But Sir Herbert was talking again. 'Lady Peters has shown us your accounts,' he said, 'and they are, while transparently honest, disturbingly amateur.' He glanced at the other board members. 'And before the situation is beyond help, I think we ought to forget our past disagreements.' He leaned forward and smiled at Eleanor, clearly certain she would see the sense in his words.

186

'Disagreements?' she burst out, quite forgetting her promise. 'You sacked me!'

'Youth and enthusiasm versus age and experience,' Sir Herbert said. He smiled at his fellow board members. 'Twas ever thus.' They laughed with him. At her. Eleanor felt her cheeks flame. She forced herself to stay in her seat, but she felt her nails bite into the palms, so hard was she clenching her fists. 'Now,' Sir Herbert said, as if nothing were amiss, 'as far as your accounts are concerned, we would help with wages and overheads.'

Too generous, Eleanor thought. She felt the beartrap opening beneath her feet. She made herself take a long, deep breath before she spoke. 'What would you want in return?'

Sir Herbert chuckled. 'My dear young lady, what could you possibly offer an historic institution such as the East London?' he asked. Well, Eleanor thought, there's the enhancement to your reputation if you're seen to be involved with a charity; and then there's the fact that you can think you've beaten me, finally, for your humiliation over Vicky's ovariectomy. 'There is nothing in this for us,' Sir Herbert said. 'But our byword is duty; and our ambition is, as ever, to serve.' The other men at the table muttered their agreement.

Eleanor found herself wondering if there were one honest man among them. Perhaps if there were a way to gain something from them without losing too much she would be a fool to turn it down. And there was the question of Mr Marsham. He had a wife and family to support. 'Wages for more staff would be wonderful,' she said. She thought of how exhausted Lady Peters had seemed lately, how it had caused them to argue. 'We are all very tired.'

Lady Peters smiled at her. 'Before anything happens, we will discuss it all.'

'Yes of course,' Sir Herbert said. 'And when you're happy, we'll take the Thrift Street Annexe under our wing…'

'An annexe?' Eleanor exclaimed. Suddenly everything was so much clearer. 'You're taking us over?'

Sir Herbert steepled his fingers. 'Protecting you. Guiding you, no more. Just as the Empire protects many a small and needy neighbour.'

'How could you let it get this far?' Eleanor demanded of Lady Peters.

'Miss Bramwell,' Doctor Marsham said.

She rounded on him. 'And you're in agreement, obviously.' She could see it all – how he would collude with Sir Herbert to get her out then quietly take over her position himself. She knew that was what Nurse Carr thought he was up to, for the woman had made no secret of the way he had been countermanding her orders in the ward.

'No,' he said.

'We must not forget your patients,' Sir Herbert said, managing to make it sound like a threat.

'My patients had no medical care at all until I opened the Thrift.' She glared at him. 'And you didn't care one jot.' She got up and stormed towards the door.

'Miss Bramwell, there's a very great deal to discuss today,' Sir Herbert said.

She turned. 'I don't want to be part of your discussions,' she said as calmly as she could. 'I want more time to think.'

She opened the door, but paused to glare at Doctor Marsham and Lady Peters. 'Time I suspect my colleagues have already had.' She went out, letting the door slam shut behind her.

Chapter 16

'But can't you see what it would mean to this place if the East London were to take it over?' Eleanor shouted. She glared at Doctor Marsham and Lady Peters. They were in the treatment room of the Thrift. The doors were shut, but she was sure that Daniel and the nurses were hovering around outside, listening. And why shouldn't they? The Thrift was their livelihood too. Besides, she was tired of being quiet and polite, and attempting to be charming. It hadn't got her very far at the meeting. 'How long do you think it would be before the patients had to pay?'

Lady Peters sat in the corner, staring at her hands.

Doctor Marsham replied, 'Sir Herbert said nothing about that.'

No, Eleanor thought; and he didn't mention the word 'annexe' till it was all but too late, either. But she knew it wasn't Doctor Marsham she had to convince. She walked over to Lady Peters.

'They come to us because we're free and approachable,' she said. Lady Peters stared up at her. She was flushed, though whether with anger or embarrassment Eleanor couldn't tell. 'We wanted to be different – not just another ward of the East London…' Eleanor, becoming more angry, whirled on Doctor Marsham and rapped out 'where working-class men are only slightly more acceptable than women. Or have you forgotten that in your eagerness to please Sir Herbert?' She walked away in a blind fury.

'Doctor Bramwell, that's really not fair,' said Doctor Marsham.

Fair? Eleanor thought. How could he talk about fairness, when all she had worked to achieve was about to be ripped away from her? She paced around the room, trying to work off some of her anger.

'Eleanor, I do wish you would think of the good that might come of this,' Lady Peters said. She fanned herself with her hand.

'We have you to do that for us,' Eleanor snapped. 'One of us at least should see this for what it is – a way for the East London to take us over!' She took a deep breath. 'We were managing well enough before – tiredness, amateur accounts and all.'

'We're barely coping,' Doctor Marsham said. 'That's all – by the skin of our teeth. We need another doctor to attend night-time emergencies, and if Sir Herbert guarantees free treatment...'

'If!' Eleanor said, exasperated at his naivety. 'If we could believe any promise from that man.' She turned. 'You know him as well as I do.'

Lady Peters stood up. 'I think I'm going home now,' she said quietly.

'Home?' Eleanor demanded. It was exactly what she should have expected: things at the Thrift were getting difficult so Lady Peters had decided to take the easiest way out she could see; and now that the conversation was turning into a real debate, she was going home where she couldn't be challenged.

'When we're in this state?'

'Sleep on it, Eleanor,' urged Lady Peters. She started to gather up her things. Doctor Marsham went to the door, ready to open it for her. 'Think about it,' Lady Peters went on. 'Talk it over between yourselves. Discuss it with your father; but I'm tired.' She made her way slowly to the door.

Eleanor snorted. 'I realize that,' she said, pursuing the older woman. 'Tired of what we're achieving here – wanting something altogether grander.'

Lady Peters turned. 'Bone tired and rather ill, actually Eleanor.' She started to pull her gloves on. 'But your compassion is touching,' she said.

Sarcasm! Eleanor thought – after all she's put us through this morning… 'If you're ill I suggest you consult your doctor,' she said. 'I'm sure he'll be only too happy to wait on you hand and foot.'

'Thank you. I will.' There was no irony in Lady Peters' tone.

It only made Eleanor angrier. 'Because', she went on, her voice getting louder as she spoke, 'that's one of the responsibilities that come when you work in a place like this – to look after yourself so that you don't let your colleagues down when they need you the most.'

Lady Peters held Eleanor's gaze for a long moment. Her expression was unreadable. Then she said, 'Mr Marsham?' He opened the door for her and she left.

Eleanor watched her go. She felt her lower lip tremble, and knew she was close to tears. If Lady Peters was ill, why hadn't she said something? She shouldn't have let it get to this stage. Doctor Marsham turned back to her.

She got up hurriedly and turned away from him so that he

wouldn't see how upset she was. 'I can't bear women who plead exhaustion as soon as there are problems,' she said. She knew she still sounded angry and wondered if he would realize how much of that was born of guilt.

'She looks ill,' he said.

'Well,' Eleanor muttered, 'Sir Herbert's her doctor. I'm sure he'll look after her.' Just the thought of him – his patronizing voice and his horrid little pats and squeezes – was enough to send a shudder through her. 'Odious man,' she said. The thought of working with him on a daily basis turned her stomach. 'But you, Mr Marsham?' she said, turning on him.

'I attended a meeting I was told to attend,' he said, holding her gaze without flinching. 'I barely opened my mouth and now you're treating me like the enemy.' He shook his head. 'Unfair, Miss Bramwell.'

He went, leaving Eleanor alone in the room. She pushed her hair back out of her eyes. She hadn't meant to get so angry with Lady Peters, Eleanor thought: but she shouldn't have gone to the East London without discussing it first. That was no excuse, though, and she knew it. She'd been downright rude; and as for failing to notice that Lady Peters was ill – well, she was a doctor. She had no excuse there, either.

And on top of all that, it seemed she had misjudged Mr Marsham also. She sighed, suddenly weary herself; but that would never do. There were patients to be seen. She went outside and started work.

***

Lady Peters came to visit that evening. Her colour was very high – it was beyond Eleanor how she'd ever mistaken it for mere anger or embarrassment – but she seemed a little more rested.

They sat in the drawing room. Lady Peters had a small glass of port, while Eleanor and her father had their usual whisky, which they sipped while Lady Peters explained that she had been to see Sir Herbert that afternoon.

'I really must obey him this time,' she said. Eleanor only hoped his diagnosis and treatment were correct. Herself, she would not have taken a sick cat to him. 'I shall recuperate in the spa for a month.' She looked at Eleanor contritely. 'After that, we can find out whether you and I can ever agree on the future of the Thrift.'

'Of course we can agree,' Eleanor said, equally contritely. 'We always do, eventually.' She sipped her whisky. 'I'll miss you,' she said.

'You'll be glad to get rid of me,' Lady Peters said. She laughed and for a moment she seemed almost her old self. 'But quite frankly I'm glad Sir Herbert is being so firm.' She looked away, obviously embarrassed. 'I do need the rest – get rid of this silly spastic colon.'

That can't be right, Eleanor thought. But it was her father who spoke. 'Is that what he said you have?'

Lady Peters nodded. 'Yes,' she muttered.

Father looked at her sharply. He seemed to come to a decision. 'Are you in pain?'

'Sometimes,' Lady Peters said. She wouldn't meet Father's eyes. 'Employ a secretary while I'm away,' she told Eleanor, obviously trying to change the subject.

'Did he examine you properly?' Father persisted.

'Well, he hardly examined me improperly, Robert,' Lady

Peters said. She smiled, and again there was the ghost of her old self. She stood up slowly and with great difficulty. Eleanor and her father got up too.

Lady Peters said, 'Take this time', she winced, 'to think very carefully about Sir Herbert's offer, and don't alienate him more than you can help.' Eleanor couldn't meet her gaze. She wouldn't make a promise she knew she couldn't keep, but she didn't want to worry Lady Peters or, worse, start another argument. 'I hope I can leave everything in your hands,' Lady Peters said.

Eleanor smiled. 'Yes of course,' she said. 'We'll amaze him with our efficiency.'

'Then I shall rest easy,' Lady Peters said. She walked towards the door.

Eleanor and her father went with her into the hall.

'Will you at least leave us an address so that we can write to you?' Eleanor asked.

Lady Peters patted her on the hand. 'Don't be so melodramatic, Eleanor,' she said. 'Of course I will. I'm not going into a nunnery!'

Eleanor smiled, finally secure again in her friendship with the older woman.

Lady Peters started to put on her jacket, which Kate was holding out for her. Before she had even put her arm in the sleeve, she gasped in pain. She stood with her arms clenched to her sides.

'Lady Peters?' Father asked. She put up her hand to shush him. 'Have you told Sir Herbert about these pains?' he said sharply.

She didn't answer, just continued to allow Kate to help her into her jacket.

Suddenly she cried out. She doubled over.

'Lady Peters!' Eleanor cried out. She rushed towards her. So did her father and Kate.

'Let's get her sitting down,' Father said.

With his support and Eleanor's, Lady Peters was able to hobble into the drawing room.

'Robert,' she said, between little gasps of pain, 'I'm so sorry.'

'No, no,' Father answered. 'Don't worry.' He caught Eleanor's eye. 'I'll send for Sir Herbert,' he said and hurried away before Lady Peters could object.

Eleanor helped Lady Peters to take her jacket off again and lie down on the sofa. 'May I examine you?' Eleanor asked, crouching down next to her.

'I don't think you'd better,' Lady Peters said. She gasped and put her hand to her side. 'It's never been quite this bad,' she said, breathless from the pain.

Eleanor's father came back into the room. 'He could be anywhere in London,' he said. 'It could take him hours to get here,' he added, coming round to where he could get a good look at Lady Peters.

'He'll be furious,' Lady Peters said. She was almost in tears.

Good, Eleanor thought; she hoped he was so furious that he stormed out of the house leaving Lady Peters in their care. If he did, it would be the first time in years Lady Peters had had a competent physician.

'At least let us get some idea of what we're dealing with,' Eleanor said.

'I agree,' Father said. Lady Peters put her hand up to her face. 'No doctor could object to that,' he added.

Lady Peters bit her lip. Finally, she nodded.

Eleanor carried out the examination. When she had finished, she went into the hall to talk to Father.

'Fever?' he asked.

Eleanor nodded. She glanced at the thermometer she was holding. 'A hundred and three degrees,' she said. Sir Herbert had missed it; but then, she herself had dismissed it.

'Sir Herbert said it was overwork,' Lady Peters called out. 'And strain.'

Father went to talk to her. Eleanor followed him. 'Distension, tenderness and pyrexia,' she said firmly, sliding the thermometer back into its case.

Father sat on the end of the sofa. 'Have you been sick at all?' he asked gently.

'I thought it was Sir Herbert's tonic,' Lady Peters murmured. 'I have been taking laudanum for the pain.'

Of course she had. She'd complained often enough about the headaches it gave her. Eleanor had never bothered to ask what she was taking it for in the first place. I was tired, she thought defensively; but she knew it would not do. 'Vermiform appendix,' she said firmly. 'I have absolutely no doubt. How Sir Herbert missed the tenderness…'

'He never examined me,' Lady Peters said. 'Not in that way.'

'A patient exhibiting acute abdominal pain, and he just talks to her!' Eleanor spat out the words as if they were poison, though she knew that, in truth, part of her anger was at herself.

'Stop it,' Lady Peters said. 'I know you don't like him…'

'Liking has nothing to do with it,' Father interrupted her. 'And to mask your symptoms with laudanum, then just send

197

you on your way.' He sighed at the awfulness of it.

'What is the matter with you Bramwells?' Lady Peters asked. Her voice was reedy with pain. 'Why must you always create problems where there are none?' She winced against the pain. 'Sir Herbert did his very best, I'm sure.'

'This is a serious condition, Cora,' Eleanor said. She had rarely used Lady Peters' Christian name; that she did so now was a sign of her worry and her desperate need to make herself understood. 'He is negligent and incompetent.'

'Oh, enough!' cried Lady Peters. 'No more criticism.' She struggled to sit upright, then sat breathless for several moments. 'It took too much hard work to get him on your side to see you throw it all away now.' She slumped back down, exhausted.

Eleanor stared down at her. Her skin was flushed and waxy, and her eyes were bloodshot. She was clearly still in great pain; and yet, thought Eleanor, she's still thinking of the Thrift – of what that damned man might be able to do for us. When all he wants is to enlarge his little empire and use us to increase his reputation.

Before she could think of a way to say that without agitating Lady Peters again, there came a tap at the door. Kate opened it without waiting for an answer. Sir Herbert pushed past her into the room.

He strode across the room to the sofa. Father stood back to make room for him.

'Lady Peters!' he cried as if he were on a social visit. 'My dear!' He bent over her and took her hand.

'Oh, I am so sorry to be such a nuisance.'

Sir Herbert sat on the end of the sofa. 'Nonsense,' he said, 'you're no such thing.' He touched her temple with the back of his hand, then looked up at Eleanor. 'What happened?'

'Nothing happened,' Eleanor replied, 'apart from the pain she's been suffering for days.'

Sir Herbert turned his attention back to Lady Peters. 'I told you to rest, my dear lady,' he chided. 'Have you been allowing yourself to become agitated?'

'No, not really,' Lady Peters said. Eleanor could almost believe she were afraid of the man's disapproval. 'We were just…agreeing to disagree.'

Sir Herbert tutted. He looked up at Eleanor, who glared back at him. 'You may thrive on discord and excitement,' he said, 'but not all ladies are the same, you know.'

Eleanor looked away. It was that or tell him exactly what she thought of him, and she feared the effect that would have on Lady Peters.

'Lady Peters has an acutely engorged appendix,' Father snapped. 'We should be preparing to operate – not discussing her emotional state.'

Sir Herbert touched Lady Peters' forehead again. 'I think I know my patient,' he said. He chuckled conspiratorially to Lady Peters, as if they shared some great secret. Then he stood up and went to his case.

'You know her?' Eleanor said. 'You don't even know what her temperature is.'

Lady Peters struggled to sit up. 'Oh, please,' she said. 'Please, Eleanor. Gentlemen.'

Father took Sir Herbert's place on the sofa. 'Lie still,' he pleaded. 'Lie still…'

'If you would,' Sir Herbert said, 'I would like to carry out my examination.' He opened his medical bag.

'At last,' Eleanor exclaimed. She left the room, and a moment later Father joined her in the hall.

While they waited, Eleanor prepared a tray of surgical instruments. 'Best to be ready,' she said as she brought them through from Father's consulting room.

He nodded.

The drawing room doors opened. Lady Peters was standing slumped by the back of the sofa. Sir Herbert picked up his medical bag and moved back to her. He proceeded to haul her along with him. She was barely moving her feet.

'What on earth are you doing?' Father demanded. 'She shouldn't be on her feet.'

'Now, you're not to fuss, Robert,' Lady Peters said. Her speech was slightly slurred.

'I've given Lady Peters a sedative,' Sir Herbert said. He guided her to a hall chair. Kate stood nearby. She looked petrified. 'And now,' he said, 'I'm taking her home to rest.' He looked at Kate. 'Her coat, if you please.' Kate got it. 'A sedative, a purgative. Leeches to reduce the congestion and we shall be as right as rain.'

Leeches, Eleanor thought. Did the man think they were living in the eighteenth century?

'I feel such a fraud,' Lady Peters said. Her cheeks and lips were colourless. Her head was weaving from side to side. 'You both look so worried.'

'We are,' Eleanor said.

'No need,' Sir Herbert said, dismissing their concerns with a wave of his hand. 'Tiphylitis,' he said and turned to Lady Peters. 'Colic,' he explained. He turned back. 'The pain's quite gone, you see.' He strolled over to Eleanor and her father, as if daring them to contradict him.

Father dared. 'I'm sorry,' he said. 'I see nothing of the sort.'

'And her temperature?' Eleanor demanded. 'Is that miraculously cured, too?'

'A good night's rest and an enema of beef tea – that's what we need here,' he said. He beamed at them.

'She needs an appendectomy,' Father insisted. 'At least try not to move her.'

Sir Herbert ignored him. 'Would you be good enough to call my carriage?'

'Sir!' Kate called. 'Doctor Bramwell!'

As they looked on, Lady Peters slumped forward then crashed out of her chair. She lay motionless on the floor.

Chapter 17

As she came up the stairs Eleanor could hear Father arguing with Sir Herbert on the upstairs landing.

'Appendectomies are rarely successful,' Sir Herbert said. He glanced into the guest room where Lady Peters lay resting. 'This colonic irritation could subside given rest and sedation.'

'The kitchen table's scrubbed,' Eleanor said once she had joined them. 'Everything's ready.'

'She's not having any operation,' Sir Herbert said. His eyes bulged out of his red face. 'Good God, are you both deaf?'

'What's the alternative?' hissed Father. He was flushed with anger himself. 'Beef tea won't save her life, nor any amount of rest.'

Eleanor stared at Sir Herbert. He had been so determined to operate on Vicky, when she didn't need it. Was it only the fact that he hadn't thought of it first that was stopping him from agreeing to the appendectomy? He was usually so keen to operate. Washerwomen, porters, clerks: they were all welcome under his knife. But he was right about one thing. Appendectomies were no sure thing. They were fraught with danger and required at the very least good nerves and a steady hand.

She had it then. 'You're afraid,' she accused him. 'You're petrified.' Of course he was. How could he risk his reputation for a dangerous operation performed on a lady of quality like Lady Peters? But that was the least of it. There was his drinking to consider.

'Don't be ridiculous,' he blustered.

'You lose twice as many patients as any other surgeon.' She couldn't keep the contempt off her face. 'It's not her nerves that concern you, it's yours!'

'Absolute rubbish,' Sir Herbert snapped. 'Be quiet!'

'Now let's keep this discussion professional,' Father said.

It was no use. Eleanor had kept too much anger pent up for too long to stop now. 'You know you're no longer fit for the work, but you're too damned greedy to admit it.'

'That's enough,' roared Sir Herbert. 'One more word and I'll sue!'

'Eleanor,' Father warned.

'You're more concerned with your reputation than with your patient.' She wished she'd said it all months ago. It might have saved poor Lady Peters so much pain. 'You're a disgrace,' she finished.

'Please…' Lady Peters' voice came from inside the bedroom. 'Please…'

Eleanor raced inside. The men followed her.

'Lady Peters, please don't alarm yourself,' Sir Herbert said. He took Eleanor by the arm and marched her across the room.

'You think you're the only jealous upstart waiting for me to make a mistake?' He glared at her then turned theatrically to the bed. 'I may well make as many as the next man, but not this one,' he declared. 'Appendectomies are foolhardy and dangerous.' Eleanor was pleased to see that Father had taken the opportunity to comfort Lady Peters without Sir Herbert's interference. Now he turned and glared thunderously at Sir Herbert. 'I will not permit you to experiment on this woman,' Sir Herbert finished grandly. He darted towards the bed. 'This dear lady,' he said, taking Lady Peters' hand.

'Cora,' Father said urgently, 'this is not an experiment.' He glared at Sir Herbert and hissed, 'We have to operate.'

Lady Peters' gaze flickered feverishly from one to the other.

'Father's right, Cora,' Eleanor said. 'We cannot afford to delay.'

'This is intolerable,' Sir Herbert said. 'She is my patient.' And that's all you care about, isn't it? Eleanor thought; never mind whether she gets the right treatment.

Sir Herbert turned back to Lady Peters. 'I'll have the groom carry you to my carriage,' he said.

'Sir Herbert,' Father said. He waited until the other man looked at him. 'I have tried very hard to be polite, but Lady Peters will not be moved in this state,' he said. His eyes blazed in the lamplight.

Sir Herbert squeezed Lady Peters' hand. 'I have been your physician for seven years,' he said. 'This operation is wild and unproved.'

'You're all so kind and concerned,' Lady Peters said. Sweat gleamed on her skin. 'Eleanor,' she said and held out her hand.

Eleanor came forward, forcing Sir Herbert to make room for her. She took Lady Peters' outstretched hand in both of her own. It was hot and shaking.

'A commode,' Lady Peters said. 'Do you have one?' Eleanor nodded.

'Father?' she said. 'If you could both just leave us?'

Sir Herbert bent over Lady Peters. 'I'll not be far away, my dear lady.' He left, followed by Eleanor's father.

Eleanor and Kate started to wheel the commode over from the far corner of the room.

Before they got very far, Lady Peters called out. 'Eleanor?' Eleanor hurried over. She perched on the bed next to Lady Peters and took her hand again. 'What will happen if I walk out with Sir Herbert and take the beef tea enema?' Lady Peters asked. She stared up at Eleanor out of eyes that seemed no more than dark pits.

Eleanor hesitated. This was what she had wanted – a chance to persuade Lady Peters without Sir Herbert there to contradict her. But now she came to the moment, it seemed far too harsh to say what must be said. Clearly, though, she had no choice.

'Your appendix is acutely inflamed,' she said. 'It's going to burst. If it does, quite simply, you'll die.'

'I see,' Lady Peters said, staring at her blankly. 'What is an appendix?'

'A tiny part of your intestine,' Eleanor said, hoping she would not be required to explain what that was as well. Lady Peters looked panic-stricken. 'You've no need of it,' Eleanor soothed her. 'You'll never miss it.'

Lady Peters laughed nervously. 'Do you really think you can save me?'

'Yes,' Eleanor said firmly, though she was far from certain.

They sat in silence for a short while. Lady Peters was clearly exhausted. Sir Herbert was right about one thing – she probably would have benefited from some rest before the operation, if only there had been time for it. It was probably the only thing he'd got right in the last fifteen years, Eleanor thought; and if he'd correctly diagnosed her, Lady Peters could perhaps have had at least a little rest.

'It never occurred to me that you were so ill,' Eleanor said.

'Nor to me!' Lady Peters muttered. 'I was just so tired after painful nights lying awake.' She tugged urgently on Eleanor's hand. 'Eleanor, how are we going to manage this without alienating Sir Herbert?'

'We can't,' Eleanor said and regretted her bluntness immediately, as she saw the panic come into Lady Peters' eyes. 'We have to forget about him and do what's right for you.' She pursed her lips. 'And forget the Thrift.'

Lady Peters tried to smile. 'I never thought I'd hear you say that.' The pain took her, and she whimpered. Eleanor tightened her grip on Lady Peters' hand. It was all she could do – let Cora know she wasn't alone. 'Oh God,' Lady Peters whispered. 'Oh. My. God.'

'Dismiss Sir Herbert, please,' begged Eleanor. 'Please. It doesn't matter who he reports us to.' She stared down at the mask-like face of her friend. 'We'll defeat him – you and I.'

Lady Peters swallowed. It seemed to cost her a terrible effort. Then she nodded.

***

Sir Herbert did not take the news well. As Eleanor brought downstairs a vase of chrysanthemums, which she had removed from the guest room, she heard him say, 'There will be consequences, Bramwell.'

Father opened the door to the outer lobby. 'I'm sure there will be, Sir Herbert,' he said. He did not sound at all concerned.

'You enticed her from my care when she was delirious and confused,' Sir Herbert said. He was wasting his time: Eleanor knew of old that expression on her father's face, and she knew how intransigent he could be. She set down he vase on the hall table. 'If she dies…' Sir Herbert said.

'If she dies,' Father cut in, 'I'll see you in the coroner's court.'

Sir Herbert stared at him for a moment, then looked away. He walked over to Eleanor. She repressed a sigh. She had rather hoped to do without speaking to him again.

'When you're young it's all so easy,' he said. 'Every day a new technique, a new machine or theory.' His tongue flicked across his lips; Eleanor thought it made him rather resemble a snake. 'Wait and see how easy it all seems in thirty years' time.'

He walked away without waiting for her reply. Perhaps he sensed that he would get none. His boots clattered on the cold tiles of the floor. Father opened the door.

'Thank you,' Sir Herbert said as he went through.

Father shut the door firmly behind him. He walked back into the inner hall and went over to Eleanor. 'An enemy for life,' he said.

Eleanor nodded. That was a problem for another day, but a problem it was sure to be. 'I've told the men to take the kitchen table upstairs. Mr Marsham is setting up now.' She'd sent a note to him while Father was still making it clear to Sir Herbert that Lady Peters' decision was irrevocable.

Father pulled out his fob watch. 'Well, you'd better start sedation now,' he said. 'We'll start at half-past twelve.'

***

Eleanor held the cup of medicine to Lady Peters' lips.

'Mmm,' she said woozily. 'I could become addicted to this mixture.' The skin round her mouth was white with it.

'Note that, Mr Marsham,' Eleanor said. She hoped it

sounded like a joke. Never had they had more need to keep up their spirits.

'We can't let the Thrift be administered by an addict, Lady Peters,' Doctor Marsham said. He was preparing the ether mask for the operation. 'We may have to bash you on the head to knock you out.'

'I feel so safe in your care,' Lady Peters murmured. 'I feel so safe in your care. I was right to let my husband's legacy go to you.'

Eleanor smiled at her. 'We think so too,' she said.

'You've taught me so much, both of you...' Lady Peters said. Her voice was becoming blurred with sleep.

'Shh,' said Eleanor. 'Go to sleep.'

She stroked Lady Peters' hand until she dozed off.

***

'When you open your eyes it will all be over,' Eleanor said as she bent over Lady Peters. While she was napping, they had covered the walls and windows in clean sheets and laid out the instruments.

Now all that remained to be done was to give Lady Peters the ether, and they could begin.

'Have you decided who's holding the knife?' Lady Peters asked. A sheet covered her from chin to feet, so that only her head showed. Doctor Marsham moved round to the head of the table, holding the ether mask.

'My father,' Eleanor said. There had never been any question about it.

He appeared at her shoulder and said, 'At your service, Madam, and raring to go.' Lady Peters' mouth trembled. 'Soon be over, dear,' Father murmured.

'My will is lodged with my solicitor,' Lady Peters whispered. 'The Thrift is yours.'

'Don't tell her that,' Doctor Marsham said cheerfully. 'You're asking for trouble.'

'You'll be back in a few weeks, bossing us all silly,' Eleanor added.

'You were right about Sir Herbert. Don't let him in the door,' Lady Peters said. The effort seemed to exhaust her.

'We won't, Cora,' Father said. He nodded to Doctor Marsham. 'Here we go.' Doctor Marsham finished preparing the ether mask. 'See you after a good long sleep,' Father finished.

'I'm frightened,' she said. Her gaze darted here and there, as if she were an animal seeking escape.

Eleanor stroked her brow, while Doctor Marsham lowered the ether mask over her nose and mouth. 'Calm, deep breaths, my lady,' he said.

Suddenly the room was filled with the long slow rasp of her breathing.

Finally, Doctor Marsham nodded to Eleanor and her father. They moved into immediate action, taking the sheet from Lady Peters' abdomen and swabbing it with lysol.

Father picked up a scalpel and made the first incision. Eleanor inserted the retractors, and for a time it seemed that everything were going smoothly.

Then Father frowned. Eleanor saw him stare at the appendix.

'Trouble?' Doctor Marsham asked.

'Damn,' Father said. He looked up. 'It's perforated.'

'Cora...' Eleanor whispered. She glanced at the woman's

face. She'd made a promise that they would save her. She only hoped she could keep it.

'Swab, please,' Father said. Eleanor wiped excess blood out of his way. 'It's going to be a long job, Marsham,' he said.

'She's got a stout heart,' Doctor Marsham answered. 'Take your time.'

It's just as well we've that on our side, Eleanor thought. It may be all we do have. She pulled on the retractors to give Father more room.

'It's just as well we didn't wait any longer,' Father said.

Eleanor fought back tears, knowing that if she had been a little more perceptive they might have operated well before the appendix had come close to rupturing.

***

When Father had finished the surgery, Eleanor sutured the wound and, with some help from Kate, moved Lady Peters into bed.

Doctor Marsham and her father both offered to take turns watching, but Eleanor refused. Sometime in the night, Lady Peters' fever would break, and she wanted to be there when it did. It has to break, she thought, as she sat in the dim light of a single gas lamp. If it doesn't, we'll lose her.

Once, Lady Peters woke up and began to thrash about. Eleanor dipped a towel in ice water and dabbed gently at her face.

'Try to lie still, my dear,' she said. 'Here – a lovely cool cloth.' She draped the towel across Lady Peters' forehead. It seemed to soothe her a little.

If the temperature would only break, she would have a chance. But if it didn't... Eleanor simply refused to think of that.

She found herself drifting off into sleep and jerked herself awake. She would have paced the room but she feared it would disturb Lady Peters. Mustn't sleep, she thought. Mustn't.

But eventually she did.

A horrible rasping noise woke her. She looked around, momentarily confused. Then she realized where she was and that the noise was the sound of Lady Peters' laboured breathing. Lady Peters' skin gleamed with flecks of sweat and the blankets over her rose and fell the tiniest bit as she breathed.

'Father!' Eleanor called. 'Mr Marsham! Could you come, please?'

It seemed to Eleanor that she stood alone for hours in the darkness, listening to that terrible wheezing noise.

At last Father and Doctor Marsham arrived. Eleanor pointed at the bed. 'I fell asleep,' she said. She could barely speak for crying.

'Once the appendix had ruptured, we had little chance,' Father said. He moved to the bedside and lifted Lady Peters' wrist to take her pulse, while Doctor Marsham hurried to get his stethoscope.

When he came back with it, he listened to her chest. 'Bracycardia.' He moved the stethoscope. 'And the lungs are congested.'

'I hope she's not in pain,' Eleanor said. Her voice shook.

'Morphine, Eleanor,' Father said. 'Let's make her end as peaceful as possible.'

Eleanor went to get it but Doctor Marsham said, 'I'll get it. You stay with her.' He got up from the bedside.

He had barely moved away when Lady Peters began to make a dreadful strangled noise. Eleanor started towards her, but the noise stopped as suddenly as it had began. The slow rise and fall of the blankets stopped. For a moment, none of them moved. Then Doctor Marsham reached over and touched the pulse point in Lady Peters' neck.

Eleanor did not need the slight shake of his head to know that Lady Peters – Cora Peters, her friend – had gone from them. She turned to Father and he held her as she wept.

***

Later, all three of them – four, if you counted Kate, who seemed as upset as anyone – gathered in the dining room. Dawn had broken, clear, cold and bright: it almost seemed to mock their grief. They had plates of food in front of them, but nobody had much appetite. Last sentence put in by Kate.

'If only we'd got to her earlier, days ago,' Doctor Marsham said.

'I should have stayed awake,' Eleanor said guiltily.

'It wouldn't have made any difference,' reassured Father. Eleanor had known he would – they had gone round and round all the what-ifs and maybes and if-onlys a dozen times. A score. 'I'll send a note to the coroner,' he added.

He looked at Eleanor, and she realized they were both pondering the same question: just how much trouble Sir Herbert was capable of causing, and whether they could hope to gather enough evidence to get him struck off.

Father stood up. 'Excuse me,' he said and left.

Kate started to clear away his place.

'We've got eight hours of surgery in front of us,' Doctor Marsham said. 'Will you manage?'

Eleanor nodded gloomily. 'We'll have to tell everyone.'

'Tell them after the operations,' Doctor Marsham advised.

'Nurse Carr and Mr Bentley may as well be composed for the day even if we're not.'

There was good sense in that. Eleanor nodded again. Then a thought struck her. 'Sir Herbert will have to be told,' she said. The thought of the man repulsed her.

'She was your patient at the end,' Doctor Marsham pointed out. 'It's none of his business. Let's tell that gentleman as little as possible about the Thrift.'

Eleanor sighed. 'When you sup with the devil, best use a long spoon.'

'Best not to sup with him at all,' Doctor Marsham said, looking at her levelly.

Eleanor looked at him, wondering how she could ever have believed he would betray her, when it was clear now that he detested Sir Herbert as much as she did. She smiled. He matched it.

***

Later, on the ward, Eleanor watched as he talked to Wilf. The lad's burn had healed up now, and there was no point keeping him any longer, broken back or not.

'Going home today, Doctor,' Wilf said.

'So you are,' Doctor Marsham said, making a note in his ledger. 'When are they coming for you?'

'Said I'd meet them at the front door, Doctor.'

That struck Eleanor as a very odd thing to say. Then she noticed that Wilf was moving. But he couldn't be.

'Come on, son,' one of the patients called. 'You can do it!'

Several of the others started clapping. Wilf almost managed to swing his legs over the edge of the bed before he collapsed back, exhausted.

'Not bad, eh Sir, for a broken back,' Wilf said.

'Very good,' Doctor Marsham said. His voice was level, but his embarrassment at his misdiagnosis was almost palpable.

'You'll be playing for Clapburn Rovers before you know it,' Daniel said approvingly. A few of the patients clapped and laughed.

'Nurse Carr,' Doctor Marsham called. 'Help him please.' He shut his ledger and walked off, stiff backed, towards the kitchen.

'You knew about this little surprise,' Eleanor said, before Nurse Carr could go to Wilf.

'Doctor Marsham was so certain he was right,' Nurse Carr said. She grinned, obviously delighted with her subterfuge.

'So was I. But sometimes the swelling goes down and mobility returns,' Eleanor said. 'Shame you had to tell him this way, in front of everyone.'

'It was just a joke, Miss,' Nurse Carr protested.

'A cruel joke,' Eleanor said. 'Mr Marsham has been up all night, as I have.' She glanced at Daniel, to make sure he was paying attention. 'Lady Peters died at five o'clock this morning.'

She walked off before she had to face their questions, and went to find Doctor Marsham. She found him in the kitchen. He wasn't doing anything, just staring at the wall.

'I'll never get their respect,' he said. 'In a big hospital like the East London I am one of a hundred doctors. I may look and sound wrong, but I can hide in the crowd.' That wasn't entirely true, Eleanor thought, remembering how Caslow – himself a mere student – had bullied him on the day of the boat race all those months ago. 'Here, I stick out like a sore thumb,' Doctor Marsham went on.

'But this is where you're needed,' Eleanor protested gently. 'You'll find someone else.'

'Mr Marsham,' Eleanor said, 'I have just lost one dear friend. I don't have so many that I can afford to lose another in the same day.'

Doctor Marsham didn't reply immediately. Eleanor never found out what, if anything, he would have said, for Nurse Carr came in.

'Doctor Marsham. Miss Bramwell,' she said, and swallowed hard. 'I'm very sorry. I'll leave the Thrift as soon as you get someone to replace me.'

'There's no need for that, Nurse,' Doctor Marsham said.

'Why does anyone have to leave?' Eleanor demanded. 'We must persevere. We have to learn to work together – for Lady Peters' sake as well as our own.' She paused. Neither of the others said anything. 'How will I fight off Sir Herbert without both of you on my side?' She looked at Nurse Carr, who nodded eventually. Then she turned to Doctor Marsham.

'If you put it in terms of fighting Sir Herbert, how can I possibly run away?' he said.

***

A few days later, Father came to see how Eleanor was getting on. He arrived just in time to see Daniel, Nurse Carr and Doctor Marsham manhandling Wilf into a wheelchair. It was obvious even from a distance that teamwork was not their best virtue.

'They're trying hard,' Eleanor said, 'but they're hardly soulmates.' She sighed.

'Well, you'll soon learn how to run staff.' Eleanor looked at Lady Peters' sentimental painting of the girl and her dog.

Eleanor had put it up in pride of place in the kitchen. 'One more thing Cora was quietly good at.'

'Well, she left you as strong as she could,' Father said. 'The legacy's yours, the buildings are yours.'

Eleanor took a deep breath. 'And the problems are mine.' She turned and walked away, remembering the first day she had entered the Thrift, and how she had felt as if she had been given the sun and the moon and the stars.

'Ah,' Father said, following her. 'The stuff of medicine.' He stood next to her, looking at the ward. 'Still, we'll manage.'

'We?' Eleanor said, startled.

'In the loosest possible sense,' Father said.

Eleanor looked at him speculatively. He smiled.

Also available from Carlton Books or by post from BOOKSERVICE BY POST, PO Box 29, Douglas, Isle of Man, IM99 1BQ, British Isles: TEL: 01624 675137 FAX: 01624 670923

Thief Takers
by Lee O'Keefe

Thief Takers
The Official Inside Story of the
Blockbuster ITV Series
by Geoff Tibballs

Kavanagh Q.C.
The Official story behind the hugely
popular ITV drama
by Geoff Tibballs

Sharpe's Story
The Making of a Hero
The Official Inside Story of the
Award-Winning ITV Drama Series
by Rachel Murrell